Kelly puzzled him.

And, yes, if he was honest, intrigued him as well.

Having watched the way she behaved toward Julian, subtly encouraging his advances, it would be easy to assume that she was an extremely sophisticated and worldly young woman who was used to using her undeniable feminine sensuality and attractiveness to get whatever she wanted from life—*whomever* she wanted.

But Brough had also observed the way she behaved toward her escort, Harry, and to his own sister, and there was no denying that, with them, she displayed a warmth, a consideration, an awareness and respect for their feelings that couldn't possibly be anything other than genuine.

One woman, two diametrically opposite types of behavior. Which of them revealed the real Kelly, and why should it be so important to him to find out?

Dear Reader,

Revenge is a very strong emotion. The need to seek it and the act of avenging a wrong-doing is very empowering. Each of the four women in this, my latest miniseries, has to learn to handle this most powerful of emotions, in her own special way.

I am aware of the dangers of people becoming blinded to everything but one single, obsessive goal. As I wrote these books, I discovered that my heroines, Kelly, Anna, Beth and Dee, all share my instincts. Like me, they desperately want to see justice done but, also like me, they come to recognize that there is an even stronger drive—love can conquer all.

These four women share a bond of friendship and it is very much in my mind when I write that you, the reader, and I, the writer, also share a very special and personal bond. I invite you to share in the lives, hopes and loves of Kelly, Anna, Beth and Dee. Through love they will discover true happiness.

Love, laughter and friendship—life holds no greater joys and I wish you all of them and more.

Penny Jordan

SWEET REVENGE *Seduction*

They wanted to get even. Instead they got...married!

Look out for Anna's story in
Lover By Deception (#2068)
Coming in December 1999 from Penny Jordan

PENNY JORDAN

The Mistress Assignment

SWEET ~~REVENGE~~ *Seduction*

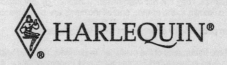

HARLEQUIN®

TORONTO • NEW YORK • LONDON
AMSTERDAM • PARIS • SYDNEY • HAMBURG
STOCKHOLM • ATHENS • TOKYO • MILAN • MADRID
PRAGUE • WARSAW • BUDAPEST • AUCKLAND

ISBN 0-373-12061-3

THE MISTRESS ASSIGNMENT

First North American Publication 1999.

Copyright © 1999 by Penny Jordan.

Visit us at www.romance.net

Printed in U.S.A.

CHAPTER ONE

'WELL, here's to Beth; let's hope that this trip to Prague is a success and that it helps her to get over that rat Julian,' Kelly Harris announced, picking up her glass of wine.

'Well, she certainly deserves *some* good luck after all that's happened,' Anna Trewayne, Beth's godmother, sighed, following suit and pausing before drinking her wine to add worriedly, 'I must admit that I feel partly to blame. If I hadn't persuaded the two of you to open your shop here in Rye-on-Averton, Beth would never have met Julian Cox in the first place.'

'There's only *one* person to blame for Beth's unhappiness,' the third member of the trio, Dee Lawson, Beth and Kelly's landlady, announced starkly, 'and that's Julian Cox. The man is a complete and utter...'

She stopped speaking momentarily, lifting her glass to her lips, her eyes darkening painfully as she quickly hid her expression from the others.

'We *all* know what he's done to Beth, how much he's hurt and humiliated her, telling her that he wanted to get engaged, encouraging her to make all those plans for their engagement party and then telling her the night before that he'd met someone else, making out that she'd misunderstood him and imagined that he'd proposed. Personally, I think that instead of bemoaning what's happened what we should be doing is thinking of some way we can punish Julian Cox for what he's done to her and make sure he can never do it again.'

5

'Punish him...?' Kelly enquired doubtfully. She and Beth had been friends from their first days together at university and Kelly had enthusiastically agreed to her friend's suggestion that they set up in business together.

'Rye-on-Averton is the kind of pretty rural English town that artists and tourists dream about, and my godmother was only saying the last time I was there that the town lacked a shop selling good-quality crystal and chinaware.'

'Us...open a shop...?' Kelly had protested a little uncertainly.

'Why not?' Beth had pressed enthusiastically, 'You were saying only last week that you weren't particularly enjoying your job. If we found the right kind of property there's no reason why you shouldn't be able to make your own designs to sell in the shop. With my retail experience I could be responsible for the buying and we could share the work in the shop.'

'It *sounds* wonderful...' Kelly had admitted, adding wryly, '*Too* wonderful... We'd need to find the right kind of premises, and it would only be on the strict understanding that we share the finances of the business equally,' she had warned her friend, knowing that although Beth had no real money of her own her grandparents were rather wealthy and Beth was their adored and adoring only grandchild.

But Beth had swept aside all her objections, and in the end Kelly had been as enthusiastic about their shared project as Beth herself.

Over the last twelve months since the shop had first opened they had gone from strength to strength and then, just over eight months ago, Beth had met Julian Cox.

He had pursued her relentlessly whilst Kelly had stood helplessly to one side and watched as her friend became more and more emotionally dependent on a man whom Kelly had never liked right from the start.

'Don't you think you're letting him rush things a little bit?' she had suggested gently, just after Beth had announced that they were getting engaged. But Beth's face had clouded and they had had their first real quarrel when she had responded uncomfortably, 'Jules said you'd say something likē that... He...he thinks that you're...that you're jealous of us, Kelly... I told him that just wasn't possible, of course...'

Jealous of them! With that comment Kelly had been forced to acknowledge that Julian Cox had very skilfully robbed her of the chance to pass on to her friend a piece of information she ought to have given her weeks before. But right now, under the influence of her second glass of the strong Italian wine the three of them had been drinking in the busy Italian wine bar where they had gone for a drink after they had seen Beth off on her buying trip to Prague, the idea of revealing Julian Cox as the unpleasant and untrustworthy character they knew him to be seemed to have taken on the air of something of a crusade, a moral crusade.

'Why should he be allowed to get away with what he's done, to walk away from his guilt in the same manner he walked away from Beth?' Dee had asked the others now.

'Walk away! What he did was even worse than that,' Kelly exploded. 'He practically forced Beth to publicly humiliate herself. I can't believe how many people seem to have fallen for the lies he's been spreading about her, implying that not only did she misunderstand his intentions but that she also actively pursued him, to the point where he was supposedly thinking of taking legal action to stop her. Bunkum! I *know* which one of them was doing the lying and it wasn't Beth. For goodness' sake, I even heard him telling her how much he loved her, how much he couldn't wait for them to be married.'

'That would have been around the time when Beth's grandfather was so seriously ill, I expect?' Dee said grimly.

Kelly looked at her in surprise, but it was Anna who answered her question first, exclaiming, 'Yes, that's right! It was when her grandfather was ill that Julian proposed.'

At thirty-seven Anna was the oldest member of the quartet. As Beth's mother's younger cousin she had just missed out on being a bridesmaid at the wedding through a serious bout of German measles. In compensation Beth's mother had asked her several years later to be one of her new baby's godparents. Only a teenager, Anna had been awed and thrilled to be considered grown-up enough for such a responsibility and it was one she had taken very seriously, her relationship with Beth even more precious to her since she and her husband had not had any children of their own.

'What's the connection between Beth's grandfather's illness and Julian's proposal of marriage?' Kelly asked Dee curiously.

'Can't you guess?' Dee responded. 'Think about it. The girl Julian dropped Beth for is known to have a substantial personal trust fund.'

Kelly made a small *moue* of distaste and looked shocked.

'You mean that Julian proposed to Beth because he thought...'

'That her grandfather would die and Beth would inherit a lot of money,' Dee finished for her. 'Yes. Once he realised that Beth's grandfather was going to recover he must have really panicked, but, of course, he met this other girl, whose inheritance is far more accessible...'

'It sounds like something out of a bad melodrama,' Kelly protested, her forehead puckering as she added, 'Besides, I thought that Julian was wealthy in his own right. He certainly gives that impression.'

'He certainly *likes* to give that impression,' Dee agreed. '*Needs* to, in fact. That's the way he draws the innocent and the naive into his web.'

Kelly's frown deepened as she listened to Dee.

At thirty, Dee was older than Kelly and Beth but younger than Anna, and the two girls had originally met her after their estate agent had suggested that they might want to look at a shop property Dee owned and wanted to let.

They had done so and had both been pleased and impressed with the swift and businesslike way in which Dee had handled the letting of her property to them. She was a woman who, although at first a little reserved and cool, and very choosy about her friends, on later acquaintance revealed a warmth and sense of humour that made her fun to be with.

Anna, who had lived in the town for the last fifteen years following the tragic death of her young husband in a sailing accident off the coast of Cornwall, had known Dee a little before Beth and Kelly had arrived on the scene. After the death of her father Dee had taken over his business affairs as well as his position on several local charities, and so was quite a well-known figure in the town.

Dee's father had been an extremely successful entrepreneur, and others in her family were members of the local farming community, and the more Kelly and Beth had come to know her, the more it had astonished them that such a stunningly attractive woman, and one whose company the male sex quite plainly enjoyed should not have a man in her life.

'Perhaps it's because she's so busy,' Beth had ventured when she and Kelly had discussed it. 'After all, neither of us have partners at the moment...'

This had been in her pre-Julian days, and Kelly had raised her eyebrows a little, reminding Beth wryly, 'We've only been in town a matter of weeks, and besides...I *saw* the look in Dee's eyes the other day when we all went out to dinner and that little girl came trotting up to talk to her—the one from the other table. Do you remember? She made an immediate beeline for Dee and it was as though the pair of them were communicating on some special wavelength that blocked out the rest of us...'

'Mmm... She *does* have a very definite rapport with children,' Beth had agreed, adding helpfully, 'Perhaps she's just not met the right man yet. She strikes me very much as a woman who would only commit herself to a relationship if she was a hundred and fifty per cent sure it was right for her.'

'Mmm...' Kelly had agreed reluctantly. 'Personally I think there must be rather more to it than that.'

'Well, maybe,' Beth had agreed. 'But I wouldn't like to be the one to pry into her past, would you?'

'No,' Kelly had agreed immediately.

Friendly though the four of them had become, and well though they all got on, there was a certain reserve about Dee, a certain sense of distance, an invisible line over which one knew instinctively one would not be encouraged to cross.

'*You* seem to know a lot more about Julian's background than the rest of us,' Kelly told Dee now.

Dee gave a dismissive shrug.

'He's...he grew up locally, and in my position one...learns things.'

Kelly's frown deepened.

'But surely if you knew his reputation was unsavoury you could have warned Beth?'

'I was away when she originally met him,' Dee reminded her, adding dryly, 'And anyway, I doubt she would have listened...'

'No, you're probably right,' Kelly agreed. 'I never liked him, but Beth was so loyal to him she wouldn't hear a word against him. It's all very well saying that we ought to do something to show him up for the rat he really is, but how can we? He's dumped poor Beth, humiliated her, and he's got clean away with it.

'I'd like to tell this new girlfriend of his just what he's like...' she continued darkly.

'It wouldn't work,' Dee warned her. 'She's as besotted with him as Beth was. No, if we're going to have any chance of getting any kind of restitution for Beth, any kind of public recognition of the way Julian lied about her as well as to her, we're going to have to use his own weakness, his own greed against him.'

'We are? But how...?' Kelly asked her curiously. Beth was such a loving, gentle, kind person, the last thing she had needed was the kind of pain and humiliation Julian had handed out to her, never mind the potential damage it could do to their own just burgeoning business. The whispering campaign Julian had so carefully and cleverly instigated when he had dropped Beth, insinuating that she had been the one pursuing him, obsessed by him, was bound to have its repercussions.

'I do hope that Beth will be all right on her own in Prague,' Anna put in anxiously, joining the conversation.

Fine-boned and very youthful-looking, Anna was, in many ways, so far as Kelly was concerned, the epitome of a slightly old-fashioned type of femininity and womanhood.

Married young and then tragically widowed, in a medieval century she would have been the type of woman who would no doubt have withdrawn to the protective security of a small convent, or perhaps in the Georgian or Victorian age she would have been the doting aunt to her siblings' large broods of noisy children.

As it was, she was apparently content with her single life, her pretty little house and her pets—a large fluffy cat and a smaller but just as fluffy dog. Her home had become for both Kelly and Beth a surrogate home from home since they had moved into the area and, whilst Kelly could never for a minute imagine Anna ever stepping into the role so vigorously occupied by her own energetic and feisty mother, there was still something very comforting and special about the gentle concern Anna showered on them both.

It was a pity she had never remarried, in Kelly's opinion, and she knew that Beth agreed with her.

'She adored Uncle Ralph; they were childhood sweethearts and they had only been married a few months when he died,' Beth had told her.

'Beth will have a wonderful time,' Dee responded robustly now. 'Prague is the most beautiful city.'

'I've heard that it's a very *romantic* city,' Anna agreed a little wistfully, or so it seemed to Kelly. 'I just hope it doesn't make her feel even worse. She's lost so much weight and looks so unhappy.'

'She'll be far too busy going round glass factories to think about anything other than business,' Dee predicted firmly.

'Mmm... It's a godsend that this trip came up when it did,' Kelly agreed. 'And that's all thanks to you, Dee. That was a brilliant idea of yours to suggest to her that we should think about buying some crystal from the Czech Republic. It's been so awful for her.

'You'd think that after what he's done to her and the way he's let her down Julian would at least have the decency to keep a low profile with his new girlfriend, but he actually seems to enjoy flaunting their relationship.'

'Like I said, the man needs teaching a lesson and being given a taste of his own medicine,' Dee reiterated. 'And if you want *my* opinion we're just the ones to do it.'

'Us...? But...' Anna started to protest uneasily.

'Why not?' Dee overruled her. 'After all, you are Beth's godmother, Kelly here is her best friend... If the three of *us* can't be relied upon to do the right thing by her...if she can't depend on *us*...then who can she depend on?' Dee said firmly.

'It sounds a good idea in theory,' Kelly allowed, moved by Dee's obvious emotion. 'But—'

'Have some more wine,' Dee interrupted her. 'There's still over half a bottle left.'

Deftly she refilled both Kelly's glass and Anna's.

'I—' Kelly started to protest but Dee cut her off.

'It's got to be finished and *I* can't have any more; I'm driving.'

It was true. It had been Dee who had taken charge when Beth had virtually collapsed after Julian had callously told her that he no longer wanted her, just as it had been Dee who had come up with the suggestion that Beth travel to Prague on a buying trip that would also hopefully take her mind off Julian and her unhappiness.

And it was Dee who had driven them all to the airport so that they could see Beth off on her journey, and now it seemed that Dee was still taking charge and making plans for them.

'So, now that we've agreed that Julian *has* to be punished and exposed for what he is, what we need to decide is *how* we're going to put our plans into action.'

She paused and then looked at Kelly before saying slowly, 'What I think would be best would be for us to punish him through his greed. You mentioned the other week, Kelly, that almost right from the first time you met him Julian was coming on to you, making overtures to you, trying to encourage you to date him behind Beth's back...'

'Yes. It's true, he was,' Kelly agreed. 'I didn't tell Beth at the time because I didn't want to hurt her and then, when it was too late, I wished I had...' She paused and then added uncertainly, 'Dee, it's all very well to *talk* about us punishing Julian for the way he's hurt her so badly, but realistically what can we do?'

Dee smiled grimly at her before turning to Anna.

'Anna, you've told us how Julian approached you for a loan, claiming that he wanted the money to use as a deposit on a house he was planning to buy for Beth and himself...'

'Yes...' Anna agreed. 'He called round out of the blue one afternoon. He said that all his cash was tied up in various investments, but that Beth had seen this house she was desperate for them to buy and he didn't want to disappoint her. He said he'd only need the money for a few months—'

'Yes, no doubt because he was expecting that by then Beth would have received her share of her grandfather's estate,' Kelly cut in angrily. 'How *could* anyone be so despicable?'

'We aren't talking about anyone,' Dee pointed out acidly. 'We're talking about Julian Cox, and Julian has a long record of very skilfully and deceitfully depriving the innocent and naive of their money—and not just their money,' Dee concluded quietly.

There was a look in her eyes that made Kelly check and study her a little woozily. The wine Kelly had drunk was beginning to make her feel distinctly light-headed, no doubt due to the fact that she hadn't had very much to eat, but she knew she was *not* imagining that unfamiliar combination of vulnerability and haunted pain in Dee's distinctive tortoiseshell-coloured eyes. Even so, there was something she still felt bound to pursue.

'If you knew just what kind of man Julian is, *why* didn't you say something to Beth?' she asked Dee for a second time.

'I told you why—because quite simply, when she first became involved with him, if you remember, I was in Northumberland nursing my aunt. By the time I'd come back and realised what was going on, how deeply she was involved with him, it was too late; she was on the verge of announcing their engagement.'

'Yes, I remember now,' Kelly acknowledged. It was true—Dee *had* been away for several months earlier in the year, looking after an elderly relative who had undergone a serious operation.

'It seems so unfair that Julian should get away with convincing everyone that poor Beth is some kind of compulsive liar as well as breaking her heart,' Anna put in quietly. 'I *know* her and I *know* she would never, could *never* behave in the way he's trying to imply.'

'He's very adept at maintaining a whiter than white

reputation for himself whilst destroying the reputations of those who are unfortunate enough to become innocently involved with him,' Dee informed them bitterly.

Kelly was feeling far too muzzy with wine to take Dee up on what she had said, but she sensed that there was some kind of past history between Julian Cox and Dee, even if she knew that Dee would not welcome any probing into it on her part.

'What we need to do,' Dee was telling them both firmly, 'is to use his own tactics against him and lure him into a position where his true nature can be exposed. It's no secret now to any of *us* that the reason he dropped Beth is because he realised that there wasn't going to be any financial benefit to him in marrying her.'

'Since we do know that, I can't help but agree with Kelly that we ought to do something to warn his new girlfriend and her family just what kind of man he is,' Anna suggested gently.

Dee shook her head. 'We know how blindly in love Beth was, and, although I hate to say this, we could all be done an untold amount of harm if Julian Cox started trying to tar us with the same brush he's used against Beth to such good effect. The *last* thing any of us needs is to be publicly branded as hysterical, over-emotional women, obsessed by some imaginary sense of injustice.'

She was right, Kelly had to acknowledge.

'Besides, if my plan works successfully, and it will, then he'll drop his current victim just as swiftly as he dropped Beth, and for very much the same reason.'

'Your *plan*? *What* plan?' Kelly asked her uneasily.

'This plan. Listen,' Dee commanded. 'We are going to mount a two-pronged attack against Julian where he's most vulnerable.

'I happen to know that one of Julian's clever little

ways of funding his expensive lifestyle is to persuade gullible people to invest in his apparently initially sound financial schemes. By the time they realise that they are anything but sound, it's too late and their money has gone.'

'But surely that's fraud?' Kelly protested. Dee shrugged her shoulders.

'Technically, yes, but Julian relies on the fact that his victims feel too embarrassed or are too timid to complain. For that reason he tends to prey on the elderly and the vulnerable, the innocently naive, too trusting and honest themselves to see what he really is until it's too late.'

'The man's a menace,' Kelly complained sharply.

'Yes, he is, and we're going to expose him as he fully deserves to be exposed,' Dee told her. 'You, Kelly, are suddenly going to become an extremely rich young woman. You have a great-uncle, previously unknown and now deceased, who has left you a considerable amount of money. This inheritance isn't something you yourself have made public, of course; in fact you refuse to talk about it—its existence is something you wish to keep a secret—but its existence has subtly filtered through the town's grapevine, at least as far as Julian's ears.

'We already know that he finds you attractive; you've told us both that he made advances to you whilst he was pretending to Beth that he loved her... All you have to do is let him believe that you're prepared to commit yourself, and, more importantly, your future to him. His own ego and greed will do the rest.'

'But I can't pretend that I've inherited money...I can't lie about something like that,' Kelly said. 'What will people think when they know?'

'Only *Julian* will ever know about your supposed inheritance,' Dee assured her. 'Just as only Julian will ever know that you are a wealthy widow and have money to spare for investment,' she told Anna.

Anna looked at her uncertainly.

'He has already tried to borrow money from me, Dee, it's true, as I've just told you both, but I'm certainly not a wealthy woman and...'

'Look, when it comes to convincing Julian that you both have financial assets that we all know simply don't exist, you can leave everything to me. I promise you that Julian is the only person who will be made aware of these imaginary fortunes.'

'But will he believe it? Surely he'll...'

'He'll believe it,' Dee assured Kelly. 'He'll believe it because he'll *want* to believe it. He needs to believe it,' she told them grimly. 'From what I've learned, his own financial position is so perilous at the moment that he'll grasp just about any straw he can to save himself.

'Once he switches his allegiance from his current girlfriend to you, Kelly, and once he tries to draw you, Anna, into one of his financial scams, we'll be able to publicly reveal him for the cheat and liar that he genuinely is...'

'It sounds plausible,' Kelly acknowledged. 'And it would certainly exonerate Beth if we could pull it off.'

'As well as preventing his current girlfriend from suffering a potential broken heart and losing *her* inheritance,' Anna supplied protectively.

'So it's agreed,' Dee slipped in quickly. 'We don't have any option but to go ahead and bring him to book.'

'No, I suppose we don't,' Kelly acknowledged.

She still wasn't totally convinced that she was going to be able to carry off the role Dee had apparently cast

for her as a wealthy heiress, but her head felt too muzzy
for her to protest properly.

There was one thing she had to say, though.

'How can you be so sure that Julian *will* drop his
current girlfriend for me?'

'He wants you, we already know that,' Dee told her
forthrightly, 'and besides, you're on your own, unpro-
tected… It's *your* money…yours to do with as you
please… His current girlfriend isn't; she's got a brother
who stands between Julian and her inheritance. Julian is
running out of credit and credibility. He won't be able
to resist the bait you're dangling, Kelly. He can't afford
to resist it.'

'The bait…' Kelly swallowed shakily. The bait Dee
was referring to, as she knew only too well, wasn't just
her imagined fortune, it was Kelly herself, and since she
personally thought that Julian Cox was the most loathsome, obnoxious, revolting and undesirable man she had
ever met…

'But if Kelly's going to pose as a wealthy heiress, then
surely Julian won't be interested in my money as well,'
Anna protested.

'Don't you believe it,' Dee corrected her. 'Julian is
greedy and avaricious; he won't pass up any opportunity
to get his hands on some extra cash.'

'But I've already refused to help him once,' Anna
pointed out.

'You're a woman; you can change your mind,' Dee
told her mock-sweetly. 'Look, you can both leave all the
details of putting our plans into action to me. All I want
from you is your agreement, your *commitment*, to help
Beth, and I *know* I can rely on both of you completely
for that… Can't I?'

Kelly and Anna exchanged uncertain looks.

'Beth is very dear to us,' Dee reminded them, looking first at Kelly and then at Anna.

'Yes. Of course…of course you can,' Anna agreed immediately.

'Yes. Of course you can,' Kelly agreed a little less confidently. Something warned her that, foolproof though Dee's plan sounded, things might not fall into place just as easily as she assumed, but her brain felt too clouded by the wine she had drunk for her to be able to formulate any determined assault on Dee's confident arguments and besides, Dee was right about one thing— she *did* feel that Julian deserved to be exposed for what he was…

For the next few minutes they continued their discussion, and as they did so Kelly's doubts as to the feasibility of Dee's plan resurfaced.

'I've got an early start in the morning, so if you don't mind we really ought to make a move,' Dee announced finally, checking her watch.

As she stood up Kelly realised dizzily just how strong the red wine she had been drinking actually was. To her relief Anna seemed equally affected by it. Of the three of them, Dee was the only one who seemed to have a properly clear head, which was just as well since she was the one doing the driving.

As she shepherded her two slightly inebriated charges out into the car park and to her car, Dee acknowledged ruefully that she would thoroughly deserve it if both of them blamed her in the morning for their thick heads— she, after all, had been the one who had kept on refilling their glasses—but she comforted herself with the knowledge that what she was doing was right; she owed it to— Her eyes closed. She must not think of the past, only the future—a future in which Julian Cox would meet the fate he so richly deserved!

She hadn't been able to believe it when she had discovered that Julian was up to his old tricks, but this time he wasn't going to get away with it. This time…this time he was going to discover to his cost just how strong and powerful a woman's desire for justice could be.

With an almost maternal concern she helped her two friends and fellow conspirators into her car. She intended to take very good care of them from now on, very good care… As they settled a little woozily into the rear seat Dee reflected that it was just as well that they couldn't read her mind and that they didn't know the truth. There had been one or two decidedly awkward moments back in the restaurant when Kelly had tried to question her, to dig a little deeper into the past, but fortunately she had managed to sidetrack her.

'Poor Beth…' Anna hiccuped mournfully as Dee started the car engine.

'Poor Beth,' Kelly agreed, blinking as she tried to clear her increasingly blurry vision.

'No, not *poor* Beth,' Dee corrected them sternly. '*Lucky* Beth. Just think how much more unhappy he could have made her if he'd waited until after they were engaged, or, even worse, until after they were married before betraying her,' Dee pointed out to them.

'It's going to be easier for her this way. If she had married him…'

Instinctively she glanced down at her own wedding ring finger. It was slightly thinner than its fellows as if once…? Then determinedly she looked away.

In the rear of the car her two fellow conspirators were succumbing to the effects of the extremely potent red wine she had deliberately fed them, their eyes closing.

She knew she ought to feel guilty about what she was doing—they were both so innocent and unaware, so unsuspicious…

CHAPTER TWO

KELLY woke up with an aching head and a dry mouth. Groaning, she rolled over and looked at the alarm clock on the bedside table.

Ten o'clock. She must have slept right through the alarm. Thank heavens it was Sunday and the shop didn't open until later than usual.

Swinging her legs out of bed, she winced as the ache in her head became a thunderous nausea-induced pounding.

It was all Dee's fault, insisting that they finish that bottle of red wine.

Dee...

Kelly froze in mid-step and then collapsed back onto the bed, groaning. What on earth had she done? She would have to telephone Dee straight away and tell her that she had changed her mind, that there was totally, absolutely, completely and utterly no way she could go through with the ludicrous plan she had agreed to last night.

Tottering towards the phone, still clasping her head, Kelly saw the answering machine light was flashing. Obediently she pressed the reply button.

'Kelly,' she heard. 'This is Dee. I'm just calling to confirm the plans we made last night. I've discovered that Julian and his new girlfriend will be attending a charity bash at Ulston House this evening. I've managed to get you a ticket and an escort—just as a bit of extra insurance. Julian is going to find you even more of an

22

irresistible challenge if he thinks you're with someone else. Remember, all you have to do is egg him on whilst playing just that little bit hard to get. I know how close you and Beth are and I know that you wouldn't dream of reneging on our plan or letting her down.

'Harry, your escort, will call for you at seven-thirty. He's my cousin, by the way, and completely to be trusted, although, of course, he knows nothing of our special plan. He thinks you just need a date for the evening because you're attending the do for business reasons. That could be the truth, incidentally—an awful lot of influential local people will be attending the dinner and the ball afterwards. Bye for now...'

What on earth did Dee think she was doing? Kelly wondered as she stared at the phone like someone in shock. And how on earth had she managed to get two tickets for that ball at such short notice? Kelly knew all about it. Those tickets were like gold dust. Not that she intended for one minute to go. Dee was taking far too much for granted and Kelly intended to tell her so. Where on earth had they put her telephone number?

Kelly winced as pain throbbed through her head. Last night's red wine had an awful lot to answer for—oh, an awful, awful lot!

Dee's number had to be somewhere and she certainly had to speak with her. Ah, there it was; she had missed it the first time in the address book. Breathing out noisily in relief, Kelly punched in Dee's telephone number.

The tell-tale delay before the call was answered warned her what was going to happen even before she heard the familiar sound of Dee's voice on the answering machine message.

'I'm sorry, I shan't be able to take your call today. Please leave your number and I'll call you back tomorrow,' Dee was announcing. Thoroughly exasperated, Kelly hung up.

Perhaps she could drive over to Dee's and persuade her that they ought to change their minds and their plans. What had seemed a reasonable plan last night, this morning seemed more like a totally implausible, not to say highly dangerous thing to do. For one thing, it went totally against all her own principles and, for another, how on earth was she supposed to give Julian Cox the impression that she found him attractive and desirable enough to want to break up his relationship with someone else when the truth was that she found him loathsome, reptilian and repulsive?

Yes, physically he was an attractive enough looking man, if you went for his boyish brand of fair-haired good looks, but looks alone had never been enough to attract Kelly, and there had been something about him, something about his attitude not just towards Beth but towards *her* as well, which had set alarm bells ringing in Kelly's head virtually from the first moment she had seen him. She had made a point of keeping out of the way whenever he was around and when they had had to meet she had kept a very cool and formal distance from him.

So how on earth was she supposed to convince him now that she suddenly found him the epitome of male sexiness?

She couldn't. She wasn't going to try. She had been a fool even to *think* of agreeing to Dee's outrageous plan, but she *had* agreed and something warned her that it wasn't going to be easy to convince Dee that she wanted to change her mind.

And if *she* backed out and Anna didn't, how was it going to look? She was, after all, Beth's best friend and, indeed, perhaps the best way of convincing Dee that her plan wouldn't work would be for her, Kelly, to show her how impossible it was going to be, by going to tonight's ball. She would be safe enough. There was no way that Julian Cox was going to repeat his attempt to come on to her, not after the way she had put him down the first time. And once she had failed to re-attract his notice Dee would surely accept that she had done her best and allow the subject to drop.

Yes, far better to do things that way than to risk offending Dee, who was, after all, only acting out of kindness and affection for Beth.

Where on earth were those wretched headache tablets? She had pulled everything out of their small medicine cabinet without finding them, and she knew she had bought some. And then she remembered she had given them to Beth, after the terrible crying jags she had had after her break-up with Julian had left her with a splitting headache. Glumly Kelly made her way to their small kitchen and filled the kettle.

The flat above the shop was on two floors; on the upper storey were hers and Beth's bedrooms and their shared bathroom, and on the lower floor was their comfortably sized living room, a small dining room and an equally small kitchen.

Outside at the rear of the property was a pretty little garden, and at the bottom of it was the workshop which Kelly had made her own territory. That was where she worked on her new designs and painted the china she had accepted as private commissions. Painting pretty porcelain pieces and enamel boxes was her speciality.

Before joining forces with Beth, Kelly had worked as a freelance from her parents' home in Scotland, supplying her pretty hand-decorated enamel boxes to an exclusive London store.

At three o'clock, with the shop still busy with both browsers and buyers, Kelly acknowledged that she was not going to be able to make time to snatch so much as a quick sandwich lunch, never mind drive over to Dee's.

Ironically this Sunday had been one of their busiest since they had opened the shop, and she had not only sold several of her more expensive pieces, she had also taken orders for seven special commissions from a Japanese visitor who had particularly liked her enamel-ware boxes.

At four o'clock, when she was gently showing the last browser out of the shop so that she could lock up, she was beginning to panic, not just about the fact that it was becoming increasingly obvious that she was going to have to go through with Dee's plans for the evening but, femalely, because she knew that she simply did not have in her wardrobe a dress suitable for such an occasion. She and Beth had ploughed every spare bit of cash they had into their business—both of them had been helped with additional loans from their bank, their parents and Beth's grandfather. Anna, too, had insisted on making them a cash gift, to, as she'd put it, 'cover any extras'. They were beginning to show a small profit, but they certainly weren't making anything like enough to warrant the purchase of expensive evening dresses.

Ordinarily, knowing she was attending such an occasion, Kelly would have done as she had done for her graduation ball and trawled the antiques shops and markets to find something she could adapt, but on this occasion there simply wasn't time, and the smartest thing she had in her wardrobe right now was the elegant dress and coat she had originally bought for her brother's wedding and which, though smart, was hardly the kind of outfit she could wear to a charity ball.

After she'd checked that she had securely locked the shop and that the alarm was switched on she made her way up to the flat. She was still finding it hard to understand what on earth had possessed her to agree to Dee's outrageous scheme last night. She was normally so careful and cautious, so in control of her life. Beth was the gentle, easily manipulated one of the two of them; *she* was far more stubborn and self-assured. Too stubborn, her brother often affectionately told her.

Certainly she knew her own mind; she was, after all, a woman of twenty-four, adult, mature, educated and motivated, a woman who, whilst she would ultimately want to have a loving partner and children, was certainly in no rush to commit herself to a relationship. The man with whom she eventually settled down would have to accept and understand that she would expect to be treated as an equal partner in their relationship, that she would expect in him the same qualities she looked for in a best friend: loyalty, honesty, a good sense of fun, someone who would share her interests and her enthusiasms, someone who would enhance her life and not, as she had seen so often happen in so many other relationships, make the kind of demands on her that would prevent her from living her life as she really wanted to live it.

'But what happens if you fall in love with someone who isn't like that?' Beth had once questioned when they had been discussing men and relationships.

'I won't,' Kelly had responded promptly.

Poor Beth. What was *she* doing right now? How was *she* feeling...? Kelly had never seen her looking so wretched or unhappy... Beth had really believed that Julian Cox loved her.

Since their break-up Kelly had heard rumours that

Beth wasn't the first woman he had treated badly. No, Beth was better off without him, Kelly decided as she went into their kitchen and filled the kettle. She gave a small shudder as she remembered the night she had returned early from a weekend visit to her parents to discover Beth almost unconscious on her bed. Taking too many sleeping tablets had been an accident, an oversight, Beth had assured her, and had pleaded with her not to tell anyone else what she had done as Kelly sat beside her hospital bed. Unwillingly, Kelly had agreed. Luckily she had found Beth in time…luckily…

Remembering that incident, Kelly slowly sipped her hot coffee. Was Dee really asking so much of her? No. She didn't relish the role she was being called upon to play—what modern woman would?—but it was only a means to an entirely justifiable and worthwhile end.

But that still didn't solve the problem of what she was going to wear. She and Beth were approximately the same size although Beth was fair-skinned and blonde, with soft, pretty grey eyes, whereas she was brunette, her skin tone much warmer, her eyes a dark purplish brown, damson—the colour of lilac wine, one besotted admirer had once called them.

The ball had been the subject of a great deal of excitement and speculation in town. It was to be the highlight of the town's social year. The de Varsey family, who owned the elegant Georgian mansion where the event was to be held, had been local landowners for the last three hundred years and, despite their cost, tickets had been snapped up and the event sold out within a week of them going on sale, which made it even more extraordinary that Dee should have been able to produce a pair at such short notice.

Kelly could remember how thrilled and excited Beth

had been when Julian had told her that he had bought tickets for the event.

'I'll have to hire something really special. This isn't just a social event for Julian, it's a very important business opportunity as well,' she had told Kelly breathlessly.

Kelly had never properly discovered just exactly what line of business it was that Julian was in. He had talked very grandly about his own financial acumen and the hugely profitable deals he had pulled off, and he certainly had spent a lot of time talking into the mobile phone he took everywhere with him. He drove a very large and very fast BMW, but lived in a surprisingly small service flat in a new and not particularly attractive apartment block on the outskirts of town.

Kelly hadn't been at all pleased when she had learned that he had suggested to Beth that she allow him to have some of his business mail addressed to their flat, but she had refrained from making too much fuss, not wanting to upset her friend.

Beth had been thrilled at the prospect of attending such a prestigious social event with him—as his fiancée; now another woman would be going there with him in Beth's place.

'Remember she could be just as much a victim of his ruthlessness as Beth was,' Dee had reminded her and Anna last night when Kelly had commented that she didn't know how any woman could date a man who she knew was supposedly committed to someone else.

If that was the case, Julian Cox deserved to be revealed as the unpleasant and untrustworthy creep that he was, for her sake as much as Beth's, Kelly acknowledged, frowning as she heard her doorbell ring.

She wasn't expecting any visitors. Although she and

Beth had made several new acquaintances since moving to the town, as yet they hadn't progressed to the stage of many close friendships. Getting up, she went downstairs to open the door that faced onto the main street.

A man was standing outside, a large box at his feet, a delivery van parked on the roadside behind him.

'Kelly Harris?' he asked her, producing a form for her to sign. 'Just sign here, please…'

'What is it?' Kelly asked him uncertainly, automatically signing the form, but he was already picking up the box and handing it over to her.

Fortunately, despite its awkward shape, the box was very light. Mystified, Kelly carried it up to the flat and then, placing it on the sitting-room floor, sat down beside it to open it.

The outer layer of strong brown paper, once removed, revealed an elegant, glossy white box. There was a letter attached to it. Opening it, Kelly quickly read it.

Dear Kelly, you'll need this to wear this evening. Good hunting! Dee.

Intrigued, Kelly opened the box and then folded back the tissue paper inside it to reveal a dress that made her catch her breath in delight.

Two layers of material, one in conker-brown, the other a toning deep, dark damson, in the sheerest silk chiffon, floated through her fingers. Picking up the dress, she hurried into the bedroom and held it against herself, studying her reflection in the full-length mirror.

In both colour and design it might have been made with her in mind, the toning shades of chiffon so perfect with her colouring that they immediately drew attention to her eyes and made them look even more dramatically pansy-dark than usual. And as for the style—the current vogue for Jane Austen-type high-waisted, floating, revealing evening dresses was one that could, in the wrong hands, look insipid and totally unflattering to anyone over the age of seventeen, but Kelly knew instinctively that this dress was far from insipid, and that its deceptively sensuous cut could never be worn by a woman who was anything less than totally at ease with herself and her sexuality. In other words, Dee couldn't have chosen a dress which would suit her more, and Kelly had no need to look at the immediately recognisable designer label attached to it to know that it must have been horrendously expensive.

Wonderingly she touched the fine chiffon. Although the dress was fully lined, the flesh colour of the lining meant that in a dimly lit room it could easily look as though she was wearing a dress that was virtually transparent.

Dee had even managed to get the size exactly right, Kelly acknowledged ruefully. Placing the dress reverently on her bed, she went back to the sitting room.

Inside the box beneath another layer of tissue paper lay a pretty matching chiffon stole and a pair of high-heeled satin sandals with a matching satin evening bag.

Dee had thought of everything, she admitted as she sat back on her heels.

Fortunately she already had some flesh-coloured underwear she could wear underneath the dress—a birthday present from her sister-in-law—and the pearls which had originally been her grandmother's and which her parents had given her on her twenty-first birthday would be perfect.

It was a dream of a dress, she acknowledged ten minutes later as she carefully hung it on a padded hanger. A dream of a dress for what could well turn out to be a nightmare of an evening.

There was no way that Julian Cox wasn't going to notice her wearing it. Although it was far too elegant and well designed ever to be described as sexy, Kelly knew even before she put it on that those soft layers of chiffon would have instant male appeal and be about as irresistible as home-made apple pie—although to a very different male appetite.

She glanced at her watch. If Dee's cousin was going to pick her up at seven-thirty she ought to think about starting to get ready. Her hair would need washing and styling if she was going to do full justice to that dress. Fortunately its length meant that it was very adaptable and easy to put up. Equally fortunately it possessed enough curl to mean that she could attempt a very similar if somewhat simpler style to that adopted by Jane Austen's heroines.

On the other side of town, someone else was also getting ready for the ball. Like Kelly, Brough Frobisher was attending it under protest. His sister had persuaded him to go, reluctantly wringing his agreement from him.

'Julian especially wants you to be there,' she had pleaded with him anxiously when he had started to refuse, adding slightly breathlessly, 'I think…that is, he's said…there's something he wants to ask you…'

Brough's heart had sunk as he'd listened to her. Initially when she had begged him to go with them to the ball he had assumed it was because her new boyfriend was looking for a backer for the new business venture he had already insisted on discussing with Brough; that had been bad enough, but now that Eve was dropping hints about Julian Cox proposing to her Brough was beginning to feel seriously alarmed.

At twenty-one Eve certainly didn't need either his approval or his authorization to get married, and at thirty-four he was mature enough to recognise that any man who married the sister whom he had been so close to since the death of their parents nearly fifteen years ago was bound, in the initial stage of their relationship, to arouse in him a certain amount of suspicion and resentment. Since their parents' death he had virtually been a surrogate father to Eve, and fathers were notoriously bad at giving up their claims to their little girls' affection in favour of another man; but, given all of that, there was still something about Julian Cox that Brough just didn't like.

The man was too sure of himself, too adroit... too...too smooth and slippery.

Eve had, after all, only known the man a matter of weeks, having initially met him quite soon after they had moved into the town.

Brough had decided that he had had enough of city life, and had sold out of the pensions management partnership he had founded, downsizing both his business and his equally hectic city social life by setting up a much smaller version of the partnership here in Rye-on-Averton.

Being a workaholic, city life—these were both fine at a certain stage in one's life. But lately Brough had begun to reflect almost enviously on the differences between his lifestyle and that enjoyed by those of his peers who had married in their late twenties and who now had wives and families.

'It's a woman who's supposed to feel her biological clock ticking away, not a man,' Eve had teased him, adding more seriously, 'I suppose it's because you virtually brought me up with Nan's help that you miss having someone to take care of.'

Perhaps she was right. Brough couldn't say; all he could say was that the prospect of living in a pretty market town which had its roots firmly secured in history had suddenly been an extremely comforting and alluring one.

As for wanting a wife and family, well, over the years he had certainly had more than his fair share of opportunities to acquire those. He was a formidably attractive man, taller than average, with a physique to match—he had played rugby for his school throughout his time at university and it showed. His close-cropped, thick, dark hair was just beginning to show a sexy hint of grey at his temples, and his almost stern expression was enlivened by the dimple indented into his chin and the laughter that illuminated the direct gaze of his dark blue eyes.

'It's not fair,' Eve had once protested. 'You got *all* our inherited share of charisma... Look at the way women are always running after you.'

'That isn't charisma,' Brough had corrected her dryly. 'That's money...'

In addition to the money both Brough and Eve had inherited from their parents, Brough's own business acumen and foresight now meant that if he had chosen to do so he could quite easily have retired and lived extremely well off his existing financial assets.

Perhaps it was his fault that Eve was as naive and unworldly as she was, he reflected a little grimly. As her brother, stand-in father and protector, he had perhaps shielded her too much from life's realities. Every instinct he possessed told him that Julian Cox simply wasn't to be trusted, but Eve wouldn't hear a word against the man.

'You don't know him like I do,' she had declared passionately when Brough had tried gently to enlighten her. 'Julian is so kind, even when people don't deserve it. When I first met him he was being stalked by this awful woman. It had gone on for months. She kept telling everyone that she was going out with him, calling round at his flat, ringing him up, following him everywhere. She even tried to arrange a fake engagement party, claiming that he'd asked her to marry him...

'But despite all the problems she'd caused him Julian told me that he just couldn't bring himself to report her to the police and that he'd tried to talk to her himself...to reason with her... He'd even taken her out to dinner a couple of times because he felt so sorry for her. But he said that he simply couldn't get through to her or make her understand that he just wasn't interested in her. In the end he said the only way to get her to accept the truth was for her to see him with me. Luckily that seems to have worked.'

When he'd heard the passionate intensity in his sister's voice Brough had known that it wouldn't be a good idea to give her his own opinion of Julian Cox. Certainly the man seemed to be very attractive to the female sex, if the number of women's names he peppered his conversation with were anything to go by.

No, he wasn't looking forward to this evening one little bit, Brough acknowledged grimly—and he owed Nan a visit as well.

Nan, their maternal grandmother, was coming up for eighty but was still fit and active and very much a part of the small Cotswold community where she lived, and thinking of her reminded Brough of something he had to do.

His grandmother had in her glass-fronted corner cabinet a delicate hand painted porcelain teapot, together with all that was left of the original service which went with it. It had been a wedding present passed on to her and Gramps by her own grandparents, and Brough knew that it was one of her long-held wishes that somehow the teaset might be completed. Brough had tried his best over the years, but it was not one of the famous or well-known makes and it had proved impossible to track down any of the missing pieces. The only avenue left to him, according to the famous china manufacturers Hartwell, whom he had visited in Staffordshire, was for him to buy new pieces of a similar style and have them hand-painted to match the antique set.

'The original manufacturers we amalgamated with produce a small range of antique china in the same style, but unfortunately we do not produce either that colour nor the intricate detail of the landscapes painted into the borders,' the sympathetic Hartwell director had told him. 'And whilst we could supply you with the correct shape of china I'm afraid that you would have to find someone else to paint it for you. Our people here have the skill but not, I'm afraid, the time, and I have to tell you that your grandmother's set would be extremely time consuming to reproduce. From what you've shown me I suspect that each of the tea plates probably carried a different allegorical figure from Greek mythology in its borders, so your painter would have to be extremely innovative as well as extremely skilled. Your best bet might be someone who already works on commission—paints and enamels and that kind of thing.'

And he had suggested to Brough that he get in touch

with a particularly gifted student they had had working with them during her university days. No one had been more surprised than Brough when he had tracked down the young woman in question only to find she lived and worked in Rye-on-Averton.

The telephone number and the young woman's name were written down on a piece of paper on his desk. First thing in the morning he intended to get in touch with her. Time was running out; his grandmother's eightieth birthday was not very far away and he desperately wanted to be able to present her with the missing items from the teaset as a surprise gift.

Although his grandmother hadn't been able to take on Eve full time after their parents' death—her husband had been very ill with Parkinson's disease at the time—she had nevertheless always been there for them, always ready to offer a wise heart and all her love whenever Brough had needed someone to turn to for advice. She had a shrewd business brain too, and she had been the one to encourage Brough to set up his first business, backing him not just emotionally but financially as well.

She still took a strong interest in current affairs, and Brough suspected she would be as dismayed by Eve's choice of suitor as he was himself.

And tonight Eve was expecting him to put aside his real feelings and to pretend that he was enjoying Julian Cox's company, and no doubt, for her sake, he would do exactly that.

Eve might be a quiet, shy young woman, but she had a very strong, stubborn streak and an equally strong sense of loyalty, especially to someone who she considered was being treated badly or unfairly. The last thing that Brough wanted to do was to arouse that stubborn female protectiveness on Julian Cox's behalf when what he was hoping was that sooner or later Eve's own intelligence would show her just what kind of man he really was.

He looked at his watch. Eve was already upstairs getting ready. First thing tomorrow he would ring this Miss Harris and make an appointment with her to discuss his grandmother's china. For now, reluctantly he acknowledged that if they weren't going to be late it was time for him to get ready.

Seven miles away from town, in the kitchen of an old house overlooking the valley below and the patchwork of fields that surrounded it, Dee Lawson turned to her cousin Harry and demanded sternly, 'You know exactly what you have to do, don't you, Harry?'

Sighing faintly, he nodded and repeated, 'To drive into town and pick Kelly up at seven-thirty and then escort her to the charity ball. If Julian Cox makes any kind of play for her I'm to act jealous but hold off from doing anything to deter him.'

'Not if, but *when*,' Dee corrected him firmly, and then added, 'And don't forget, no matter what happens or how hard Julian pushes, you must make sure you escort Kelly safely back to the flat.'

'You really ought to do something about those maternal instincts of yours,' Harry told her, and then stopped abruptly, flushing self-consciously as he apologised awkwardly, 'Sorry, Dee, I forgot; I didn't mean...'

'It's all right,' she responded coolly, her face obscured by her long honey-blonde hair.

Seven years his senior, Dee had always been someone Harry was just a little bit in awe of.

Dee's father and his had been brothers, and Dee had been a regular visitor to the family farm when Harry had been growing up. It had surprised him a little that she had chosen to continue her career in such a small, sleepy place as Rye-on-Averton after her father's death. But then Dee had never been predictable or particularly easy to understand. She was a woman who kept her own counsel and was strong-willed and highly intelligent, with the kind of business brain and aptitude for making money that Harry often wished he shared.

There had only been one occasion that Harry could recall when Dee had found herself in a situation over which she did not have full control, a situation where her emotions had overruled her brain, but any kind of reference—no matter how slight—to that particular subject was completely taboo, and Harry would certainly not have dared to refer to it. As well as being in awe of his older cousin, it had to be said that there were times when he was almost, if not afraid of her, then certainly extremely unwilling to arouse her ire.

'Kelly will be expecting you. You'll like her,' Dee informed him, adding almost inconsequentially, 'She'd fit in very well here, and your mother…'

'My mother wants me to marry and produce a clutch of grandchildren—yes, I know,' Harry agreed wryly, before daring to point out, 'You're older than me, Dee, and you still haven't married. Perhaps we're a family who don't…'

'It's hardly the same thing,' Dee reproved him. 'You have the farm to think of. It's been passed down in the family for over four hundred years. Of course you'll marry.'

Of course he would, but when he was ready and, please God, to someone he chose for himself. Although he tried desperately to hide it, considering that such idealism was not proper for a modern farmer, Harry was a romantic, a man who wanted desperately to fall deeply and completely in love. So far, though, he had not met anyone who stirred such deep and intense emotions within him.

CHAPTER THREE

VERY gently Kelly fingered the soft silk of her gown. Once on it suited her even more perfectly than she had expected, the colour of the chiffon doing impossibly glamorous things for her colouring.

As she looked up she saw that Dee's cousin Harry was watching her rather anxiously. She smiled reassuringly at him as they waited in the receiving line to be greeted by their host and hostess. She had known from the moment he arrived to pick her up that she was going to like Harry. He was that kind of man—solid, dependable, reassuring, as comfortable as a familiar solid armchair, with the kind of down-to-earth, healthy good looks that typified a certain type of very English male. Just having him standing there beside her made her feel not merely remarkably better about the scheme which Dee had dreamt up but somehow extraordinarily feminine and protected. It was rather a novel sensation for Kelly, who had never been the type of woman to feel that she needed a man to lean on in any shape or form.

'That colour really suits you,' Harry told her earnestly as he arched his neck a little uncomfortably, as though he longed to be free of the restriction of his formal dinner suit.

'Dee chose it,' Kelly informed him, adding truthfully, 'I feel rather like Cinderella being equipped for the ball by her fairy godmother... Although...' She paused and then stopped. There was no point in discussing with Harry her doubts about what she was doing.

41

They had reached the line-up of dignitaries now. Kelly smiled mischievously as she caught the discreetly admiring second look the Lord Lieutenant of the county gave her before he shook her hand.

It's all right, it's not me, it's the dress, she wanted to reassure his rather austere-looking wife, but then, remembering her new role as a *femme fatale*, instead she gave him a demure little smile plus a wickedly sultry look from beneath lowered lashes. It worked… His Lordship might be close on sixty, but there was no doubt that he was still a very virile man—at least if the look he was giving her was anything to go by.

Perhaps the evening wasn't going to be so much of a challenge to her thespian talents as she had originally believed, Kelly mused as they passed down the line and then turned to accept a glass of champagne from one of the hovering waiters.

As Kelly already knew, the tickets for the ball had been unbelievably expensive, with only a relatively small number available, but, as she glanced appreciatively at her surroundings, she could well understand why.

Instead of more conventionally attaching a large marquee to the house to accommodate the event, guests were allowed to wander at will through the elegant antique-furnished reception rooms. Her own Regency-inspired dress couldn't have been more felicitously in keeping with the decor, Kelly recognised, her attention caught by a pretty inlaid Chinese lacquered cabinet in one corner of the room, its shelves filled with what she suspected were Sèvres figurines.

Touching Harry's arm, she pointed it out to him.

'I'd like to go over and have a closer look,' she told him. Nodding, Harry gallantly forged ahead to make a pathway through the throng of people now filling the hallway.

Kelly had almost reached her destination when abruptly she stopped dead. There, not a dozen feet away from her, stood Julian Cox. He hadn't seen her as yet. He was busy talking with a pretty fair-haired young woman standing with him. In looks she was very similar to Beth, Kelly recognised, and she looked somehow as though she too possessed the same gentleness of nature that so characterised her best friend.

She doubted very much that that same description could be applied to the man standing on the opposite side of her. Tall, with incredibly powerful shoulders and frowning heavily, he looked extremely formidable and extremely masculine, Kelly recognised as her heart gave a sudden unsteady lurch against her ribs and her breathing quickened idiotically.

As though—impossibly, surely—he was somehow aware of her attention, he turned his head, seemingly focusing fiercely on her.

Kelly's heart gave another and even sharper lurch. He had the most intensely dark blue eyes, and such a penetrating gaze that she felt almost as though he could see right into her soul.

Now she *was* being ridiculous, she told herself stoutly, firmly assuring herself that there was no way that either he or anyone else could have guessed what was going through her mind as she looked at him. And anyway, she reminded herself as she determinedly looked away from him, she was not here to start fantasising about the admittedly very interesting sensual allure of an unknown man; she was here for a very specific purpose, and that did *not* include allowing herself to be side-tracked by anyone or anything—not even her own still very disturbed heartbeat.

Even so, she managed to sneak a second brief glance at him, and she wished she had not done so as she saw the tender and protective way in which he was bending towards the soft-featured blonde girl who was standing close to Julian. Was she, as Kelly had first assumed, the new woman in Julian's life, or was the other man her partner? Had those magnetic blue eyes that had focused on her so directly and so immediately been giving a stern warning that he was *not* available to any other woman, rather than conveying a virile, masculine awareness of her female curiosity?

Well, no doubt before the evening was over she was going to find out, she reminded herself. Julian had not seen her yet, but... She took a deep breath and started to move discreetly into his line of vision.

'Are you okay?' she heard Harry asking her in concern. 'You look a bit flushed. It's pretty crowded in here and hot...'

Rather guiltily Kelly gave him a reassuring smile. Any heat flushing her face had rather more to do with her emotional and physical reaction to the sexily masculine good looks of the man standing with Julian Cox than with the heat of the room.

Irritatingly, Julian had now turned away to talk to someone so that she was out of his line of vision. Boldly she deliberately changed direction, plunging through the crowd in order to bring herself back into it and, in the process, losing Harry, who became separated from her by the busy throng.

Julian might not be aware of her presence, she recognised after a discreet glance in the trio's direction, but *he*, whoever *he* was, most certainly was. Slightly breath-

lessly she instinctively curled her toes, and a delicious
thrill of feminine reaction ran through her as she realised
just how intently she was being studied. Sternly she reminded herself of just why she was here and the role
she had to play. The temptation to abandon it and to
revert to her normal self beckoned treacherously. She
had never been a flirt, never been the kind of woman to
go all out deliberately to attract a man's attention—she
had never needed to and she had certainly never wanted
to!

But, almost as though it was fate, just as she was
wavering, a direct pathway opened up between her and
Julian. Sternly she made herself take it.

'Julian... How lovely to see you...'

Had she got the note of flirtatious invitation in her
voice pitched correctly? Anxiously she held her breath
as Julian turned his head to look at her, wariness giving
way to a look of lustful male appreciation as she continued to smile at him.

'Kelly! What a surprise...'

'A pleasant one, I hope.' Kelly pouted, deliberately
stepping closer to him, angling her body so that she was
placing herself with her back to the blonde girl standing
silently at Julian's side and thereby excluding her from
their conversation.

'I thought for a moment that you'd forgotten me...'

'Impossible,' Julian assured her with heavy flirtatious-
ness, his glance deliberately and meaningfully lingering
on her body.

Really, he was a total creep, Kelly decided.

'Here on your own?' Julian quizzed her.

Throwing back her head, Kelly gave a small, sexy
laugh.

'Of course not,' she chided him, her voice and the

look she gave him emphasising that *she* was the type of woman who would *never* be without a male escort.

'You're looking very well,' she praised him, adding purringly, 'Very well…'

'Then that makes two of us,' Julian told her smoothly.

'Julian, I think it's time we started to make our way to the table.'

The cool, authoritative male voice intruding on their conversation caused Kelly to turn her head to look at its owner.

Close up he was even more sizzlingly sensual than she had first imagined. It must be the new persona she had assumed that was making her aware of him in such a very intimate and sexual way, she decided dizzily as her glance slid helplessly from the dark watchfulness of his eyes to his very sensual mouth. Certainly she could never remember an occasion previously when she had been so immediately and so shockingly physically aware of a man's sexuality.

'Oh, must you go so soon?' She pouted again, a little disconcerted to recognise how easily both the pout and the teasing but deliberately flirtatious glance she had given Julian's companion came to her. 'We haven't even been introduced…'

She could sense Julian's surprise at the way she was behaving, and managed to hide her own reservation at her unfamiliar behaviour. Kelly could sense Julian's reluctance to comply with her request, but his companion was already saying with a steely, not to say with a grim note in his voice, 'Yes, Julian, *do* introduce us to your friend…'

'Er… Eve, Brough, may I introduce you to an old friend—Kelly? Kelly, please meet Eve and her brother, Brough Frobisher.'

While Kelly waited for him to expand a little more on the relationship between the other couple and himself she could see from the look in Brough Frobisher's eyes that he was decidedly unimpressed by her flirtatious manner.

At least she had had one of her questions answered, she acknowledged as Harry finally arrived at her side just as Brough was determinedly turning away from her.

Eve and her *brother*, Julian had said.

Ridiculous to feel that dizzying surge of excitement and relief just because Brough Frobisher appeared to be unattached.

'We're on table twelve,' Harry was informing her as he manfully forged a pathway for them both through the press of people making their way towards the banqueting room.

Table twelve was well positioned, with a good view of the top table and close enough to the long row of French windows which opened out onto the terrace to offer the comfort of a cool walk along it should one wish to avail oneself of such a facility.

Curiously, though, as they approached the table a small altercation appeared to be taking place there between a harassed-looking couple, the man red-faced and plainly angry whilst his wife looked flushed and embarrassed.

'*You* told me we were on table twelve,' he was saying to her as Harry and Kelly approached.

'And so we were... At least, that was what Sophie said...' his wife was responding, adding helplessly, 'She must have got it wrong. You'll have to go back and check the table plan.'

As she watched the hapless couple making their way back to the entrance to the room, Kelly couldn't help feeling a little bit guilty. *Was* she being overly suspicious in suspecting Dee's magical sleight of hand might somehow be responsible for their missing seats, especially when she could quite plainly see from where she stood that the place cards the couple had been studying with such bewilderment bore hers and Harry's name?

A middle-aged couple and their daughter, the Fortescues, Kelly realised, were taking their places at the table, and another couple were taking their seats opposite Harry's and Kelly's own, which left three spare seats to Kelly's left. Discreetly she leaned across to study the place cards, her heart thumping just a little bit too fast as she read, 'Mr Julian Cox, Miss Eve Frobisher, Mr Brough Frobisher.' She had no idea just how Dee had managed to get them seated next to Julian, nor did she wish to be enlightened. Dee was turning out to be a master tactician, an expert in the art of gamesmanship and subterfuge.

'Kelly, you're on our table! What a coincidence!' Julian was exclaiming with very evident pleasure as he walked up.

Demurely Kelly said nothing, instead simply smiling at him from beneath down-swept lashes.

Half an hour later, when they had all been served with their main courses, Kelly acknowledged that Julian was even less likeable than she had previously guessed. Ignoring his girlfriend to flirt with her, he had progressed from blatantly sexually motivated compliments to the kind of sensual innuendo which Kelly found teeth-grittingly unwelcome.

Her conscience overcoming her sense of duty, she leaned across the table to ask Eve gently how long she had been living in the town and if she liked it.

'It's very pretty,' was her slightly hesitant response, and Kelly didn't miss the way she looked first at her brother before replying to her, as though seeking either his support or his approval.

Kelly felt distinctly sorry for her. She was no match for a man of Julian's unwholesome calibre, that much was more than evident to her, and Kelly hadn't missed the way she had bitten her lip once or twice when Julian's compliments to herself had pointedly underlined just how sexually attractive he found her.

'What do you do?' Kelly asked her, trying to draw her out a little, but it seemed she had asked the wrong question because immediately the younger woman flushed and looked helplessly at her brother before replying.

'Oh, nothing... I'm afraid my art degree isn't... doesn't...'

Her voice trailed away and Julian cut in boastfully, 'Eve doesn't need to work, do you, my sweet? She has her own income...a trust fund...'

As he spoke he reached for her hand and squeezed it, lifting it to his lips to kiss her fingers in what Kelly considered to be an excessively exaggerated and insincere manner, but to judge from the pretty pink blush that coloured Eve's pale skin she didn't seem to find anything wrong with his manner towards her.

What would she say, Kelly wondered grimly, if she knew that whilst he was kissing her fingers his other hand was resting meaningfully on Kelly's chiffon-clad knee, and she had in fact just had to edge determinedly away from him to stop him from rubbing his leg potentially even more intimately against hers?

He really was totally repulsive, Kelly acknowledged with repugnance as she started to turn towards Harry, stopping when unexpectedly Brough Frobisher entered the conversation, telling her coolly, 'As a matter of fact, Eve works for me. What about you? What do you do?'

Before Kelly could answer him, the Master of Ceremonies called on them for silence whilst their host made a speech.

Gratefully Kelly got to her feet, glad to have the opportunity to shake off Julian's wandering hand. Her dislike of him was growing by the minute—and not just on her own behalf. The minute Julian had mentioned Eve's trust fund Kelly had immediately been aware from his avaricious expression just where the other girl's attraction for him lay. Poor thing, like Beth before her she was obviously too unworldly and naive to see through him, but surely her brother *must* be able to recognise just what Julian was like.

Although he had listened in silence to Julian's conversation throughout the meal, more of an observer than a participator, Kelly had been keenly aware of the intensity of his silent scrutiny of them all. *Was* she being over-sensitive in thinking that he had been particularly watchful where *she* was concerned? At one point, just before the Master of Ceremonies had provided his welcome diversion, Kelly had actually felt as though Brough Frobisher's gaze was somehow burning a laser-like beam right through the table to where Julian's hand was resting on her leg. Not that she had wanted it to be there. She gave a small shudder. He repulsed her now even more than he had done before.

'I can't encourage him. I don't like him. He's loathsome,' she had protested despairingly to Dee last night.

'All you have to do is let him *think* that you're interested in him,' Dee had soothed her. 'All we need is for him to show himself in his true colours so that we can...'

'So that we can *what*?' Kelly had pounced, but Dee had simply given her a mysterious smile.

The speeches were almost over; the Master of Ceremonies had announced that there would be dancing in the ballroom. Hopefully then she would be able to escape Julian's unwelcome attentions, since he would be duty-bound to dance with Eve.

'Your lipstick's all gone and your hair needs brushing,' she heard Julian saying critically to Eve as the speaker sat down.

'I'm afraid Eve doesn't really have much idea about how to dress properly. She isn't into designer clothes. I dare say you didn't have much change out of a thousand pounds when you bought yours?' he questioned, and Kelly knew from the look in his eyes that the news of her supposed inheritance had already reached him via that mysterious 'grapevine' Dee seemed to know so much about. As he spoke Julian's glance slid from Kelly's eyes to her mouth, and he murmured in a much lower voice, 'Mind you, one has to admit the poor darling doesn't exactly have the right kind of raw material...unlike you... Has anyone ever told you that you have the most amazingly sexy eyes...and mouth...?'

Kelly had to fight to suppress the dark tide of colour threatening to betray her feelings. It wasn't embarrassment that was driving the hot blood up under her skin, but anger. How dared he behave so insultingly towards his girlfriend? No wonder she was looking so unhappy. But that was no reason for her brother to give her, Kelly, such a contemptuously angry look. *She* wasn't the one who was responsible for Eve's humiliation.

'I was just going to go to the Ladies to tidy up myself,' she fibbed, smiling warmly at Eve. 'Do you want to come with me?'

'Oh, yes...'

Smiling with relief, Eve got up to accompany her.

'Have you known Julian long?' she asked Kelly shyly as they stood side by side in the elegantly decorated cloakroom, studying their reflections in the mirrors in front of them.

'Mmm...quite a while,' Kelly responded.

'He's a very special person, isn't he?' Eve enthused, her eyes shining with emotion, her expression betraying just how deeply involved with him she was.

Kelly's tender heart ached for her, and she only just managed to resist the impulse to tell her exactly what she thought of Julian Cox and why. Instead she asked, 'What about you? Have *you* known him long?'

'Er, no...not really... That is...' She paused and then said in a breathless rush, 'He's asked me to marry him. Everything's happened so quickly between us that I still can't quite... It's quite a frightening feeling when you fall in love, isn't it?' she asked Kelly with a small, poignant smile. 'This is the first time that I... Brough thinks it's too soon... Julian gets quite cross with me sometimes because he thinks I rely too much on Brough, but he's taken care of me ever since our parents died and...

'I haven't met many of Julian's friends yet,' she confided, changing the subject slightly. 'Julian says that he wants to keep me...us...to himself for a little while...' She smiled and blushed. 'He's so very romantic and loving.'

Oh, yes, Kelly wanted to agree sarcastically. So very romantic and loving that he broke my best friend's heart, just the same way he is probably going to break yours. But caution made her hold her tongue.

How much did Eve know about Julian's relationship with Beth?

Along with the revulsion and dislike Julian had aroused within her was a growing sense of anger and an unexpected surge of desire to protect Eve from suffering the same fate as Beth. Perhaps she herself was a rather stronger and more determined character than she had previously realised, Kelly acknowledged. With every word that Eve spoke she could feel an increasing awareness of how right Dee was to want to have Julian exposed in his true colours, and an increasing desire to help achieve that goal, even if it meant putting herself in an unpleasant, but thankfully temporary, position. Much as it went against the grain with her to subtly encourage Julian's amorous advances, much as she disliked the role she was being called upon to play, there was a real purpose to it.

Checking her own freshly applied lipstick, she gave Eve a warm smile.

'Don't let Julian bully you,' she advised her.

The younger girl's face went scarlet.

'Oh, he doesn't. He isn't... It's just that he's used to women who are so very much more glamorous than me and of course he wants...expects...'

'If he loves you then he must love you just the way you are,' Kelly pointed out, but she could see from Eve's expression that she did not want to hear what Kelly was trying to say.

Perhaps when she saw exactly what kind of man Julian really was she'd realise just how unworthy of her love he was. Kelly certainly hoped so.

Brough frowned thoughtfully as he watched his sister and Kelly weaving their way back through the crowd to their table. Kelly puzzled him and, yes, if he was honest, intrigued him as well.

Having watched the way she behaved towards Julian, subtly encouraging his advances, it would be easy to assume that she was an extremely sophisticated and worldly young woman who was used to using her undeniable feminine sensuality and attractiveness to get whatever she wanted from life—*whoever* she wanted from life, regardless of whether or not the man in question was attached to someone else. But Brough had also observed the way she behaved towards her escort, Harry, and to his own sister, and there was no denying that with them she displayed a warmth, a consideration, an awareness and respect for their feelings that couldn't possibly be anything other than genuine.

One woman, two diametrically opposite types of behaviour. Which of them revealed the real Kelly, and why should it be so important to him to find out? Not, surely, just because the man she was making a play for was the same man her sister claimed to be in love with? After all, there was nothing he wanted more than for something, someone, to make his sister see just how unworthy of her Julian Cox actually was.

Discreetly he studied Kelly. Her dress was expensive, and fitted her as though it had been made for her, but something, some experienced male instinct, told him that she was not quite so comfortable and at home in it as she wanted others to believe. Every now and again she gave a betraying glance down at herself, rather in the manner of a little girl uncertain of the wisdom of wearing her mother's borrowed clothes. As Julian had so admiringly pointed out, she was immaculately groomed, but personally Brough would have rather liked to see her dressed casually in jeans, her skin free of make-up, her wonderful hair soft and tousled and her even more wonderful eyes and mouth...

His eyebrows snapped grimly together as he recognised the direction his thoughts were taking. It was a long time since a woman had attracted him as powerfully or as immediately as Kelly—or as dangerously. On two counts. If she *was* the type of woman she was portraying to attract Julian Cox's attention, then she was most decidedly not *his* type. And if she wasn't...if that unexpected and alluringly enticing chink of vulnerability and uncertainty he had so briefly glimpsed beneath the sophisticated image she was trying to portray was the real Kelly...then that would make it even more imperative that he didn't involve himself in any way with her. His life was already complicated enough as it was, with Eve. One day he would marry, settle down, with a nice, calm, sensible girl—a woman who did not pretend to be something she wasn't.

Of course, there was one way he could probably find out just what sort of woman Kelly really was. The way a woman responded, reacted, to a man's first kiss could say an awful lot about just what kind of person she was, Brough mused.

His frown deepened. What on earth was he thinking? There was no way he could justify that kind of behaviour—or those kinds of thoughts.

His last serious relationship had been when he was in his very early twenties. He had thought himself in love—had thought that she loved him. They had met at university and then she had taken a year out to travel while Brough had stayed at home to be near Eve. When they had met up again both of them had been forced to acknowledge that whatever they'd had had gone.

Since then he had dated...there had been women...but

by the time he had reached thirty he had decided that he must be the kind of man in whom logic and responsibility always won out over passion and impetuosity. And so he was...wasn't he?

'I want to dance with you.' Kelly's heart sank as she saw from the loaded, explicitly sexual way that Julian was regarding her as he spoke to her just how successful Dee's plan had been. There was no doubt just what was on Julian's mind, even without the heavy, lingering glance he gave her breasts.

He was being too obvious, too potentially hurtful to Eve and insulting towards her, Kelly decided as she shook her head and reminded him, 'You haven't danced with Eve yet...'

'I don't want to dance with *her*; I want to dance with *you*,' Julian insisted as he reached out to raise her from her seat.

Unhappily Kelly fought her conscience. This was too much, and inexcusable. Just how much wine had Julian had to drink? she wondered uneasily, wishing that Harry hadn't chosen just that moment to disappear.

'Kelly has already promised this dance to me.'

The interruption from Brough Frobisher was just as unexpected as his coolly uttered, authoritative fib.

Without allowing Julian the opportunity either to protest or argue, Brough came over to her, holding out his hand. Shakily Kelly stood up. She didn't particularly want to dance with him, but dancing with him was infinitely preferable to having to dance with Julian.

Good manners suggested that she ought to thank Brough Frobisher for rescuing her, but to do so would surely be to step out of the role Dee had cast for her and, perhaps even worse, to give him the opportunity to point out that she herself had been actively encouraging Julian to believe that she was interested in him.

'Your sister is very sweet,' she commented awkwardly as Brough led her onto the floor.

'Sweet?' His dark eyebrows lifted as he gave her an appraising look. 'An excess of sweetness can be unpleasantly cloying. I don't consider her to be sweet, rather a little too naive and vulnerable. How long have you known Cox?'

His abrupt question caught her off guard.

'Er...a while... He...we're old friends,' she stammered, boldly remembering her role.

'Old *friends*,' he repeated, stressing the word as he looked hard at her. 'I see.'

Kelly hoped devoutly that he did no such thing.

As they reached the dance floor he touched her lightly on the arm, turning her expertly towards him. The band was playing a slow, intimate dance number, and immediately she felt his arm go round her Kelly tensed.

It wasn't that she wasn't used to dancing in close proximity to a man, it was just that somehow it was unnerving with *this* man—

'Enlighten me,' he was saying to her. 'What exactly is it about Cox that quite patently makes him so attractive to your sex?'

Kelly glanced warily up at him. He was immaculately dressed and she could just catch the scent of the very masculine cologne he was wearing, she noted approvingly. Julian's apparent addiction to very strong and no doubt trendy aftershave was not to her personal taste at all. But despite Brough's elegant grooming she suspected that without the shave he must have had before coming out this evening his very thick and very dark hair must mean that most evenings his jaw must be shadowed and slightly rough to the touch, adding a delicious extra frisson of sensuality to being kissed by him, especially if you were a woman who, like her, possessed slightly sensitive skin.

Appalled by the direction of her own unruly thoughts, Kelly realised that she had still not answered his question.

'Er...Julian likes women,' she told him lamely.

Immediately his eyebrows rose.

'He certainly does,' he agreed silkily. 'Doesn't that bother you? In my experience, most women prize loyalty and exclusivity in a relationship...'

'Julian is simply a friend,' Kelly reminded him sharply.

'A very intimate friend?' Brough pressed.

He was digging too deep, questioning her too closely, Kelly recognised, and in order to answer him she was either going to have to commit herself to more lies or risk betraying the fiction she was creating.

'It's hot in here,' she complained, pulling free of him. 'I need some fresh air.'

It wasn't entirely untrue; she *was* hot and the terrace she could see beyond the ballroom's open French windows did offer a much needed escape from the cause of that heat—which was not so much the air in the ballroom as the presence of the man beside her and her own feelings of trepidation and guilt.

As she headed for the terrace, it didn't occur to Kelly that he would follow her. She could guess from the way he had been questioning her just what he thought of her, and she knew that in refusing to answer him she had equally plainly confirmed those suspicions.

It was a relief to reach the cool shadows of the terrace, and, avoiding the other couples strolling its length, Kelly turned instead to descend the flight of stone steps that led into the garden.

She was almost at the bottom when a sharp stone underfoot caused her to stumble, but instead of experiencing the ignominy of falling to her knees on the gravel pathway she was scooped up in a pair of hard male arms and she heard Brough's voice against her ear telling her calmly, 'It's all right, I've got you...'

He certainly had, and it seemed he had no intention of letting her go, either. Against her body she could feel the heavy thud of his heartbeat as he helped her to her feet but still continued to hold onto her. Disconcertingly her own heart suddenly started to race, and she discovered that she was finding it hard to breathe.

'Did you twist your ankle? Can you put your weight on it?'

'My ankle...' Dizzily Kelly looked up into his eyes, and then at his mouth, and then foolishly she did exactly the same thing again. The effect on her nervous system was like a shock wave of mega-force, a subterranean uprising of such intensity that it blew every fuse on her internal alarm system—and then some.

Unwisely she licked her inexplicably dry lips. What had he said about her ankle? What ankle? Helplessly her gaze clung to his. Surely no man should have such ridiculously long lashes, such darkly intense eyes. She felt as though...as though...

'Kelly. Kelly...'

'Yes,' she whispered in tacit acknowledgement of what she knew was going to happen.

A kiss was simply a kiss...wasn't it? How could she be so foolish, so unaware...so naive as to think *that*? *This* was certainly no mere kiss, this meeting, caressing of her mouth by and with his. But even as she tried to analyse what was happening, to hold onto some protective shred of sanity, the thread holding her, it snapped beneath the weight of what she was feeling. Blissfully she gave herself up to sensation—to the smooth, rough, hot, sweet feel of his mouth against hers, to the swift ascent from careful, hesitant exploration to the dizzying heights of a complete and passionate explosion of need she could feel shaking her body.

'Kelly!' As he whispered her name Brough's hand reached out to touch her face, to stroke tenderly along her jaw, to support her head as his tongue-tip parted her sensuously swollen lips.

'Brough!'

Was that really her whispering his name in a sigh that was all soft yearning and longing, exposing dangerously the tender, vulnerable heart of herself which she normally kept so carefully guarded?

Unable to stop herself, Kelly reached out and touched his jaw with her fingertips. His skin felt cool and strong. Hard, masculine. Shivering in pleasure, she stood still beneath his kiss. His arms tightened around her almost as though he wanted to guard and protect her.

Shyly Kelly opened her eyes, unable to resist the temptation to look at him whilst he was caressing her mouth with the most unbelievably erotic brush of his lips against hers, but to her shock his own eyes were open and he was looking right back at her.

The sensation of looking so deeply into his eyes whilst he kissed her felt like the most intimate experience she had ever had. Her earlier shivers had become deep tremors of intense emotion, and when he stopped kissing her and raised his mouth from hers to look searchingly at her Kelly made a small sound of distress, her fingertips touching his lips in a gesture of silent longing.

This time it was *his* turn to shudder, racked by a surge of male desire so strong and so open that Kelly felt her own body start to respond to it—to it and to him.

This time, when they kissed, she couldn't remain passive beneath his mouth, but returned each caress, mirroring every touch, every sound as they kissed and broke apart, only to kiss again.

'Kelly, are you out there?'

The sound of Harry's worried voice from the terrace above them brought Kelly back to reality. Hot-faced, she stepped back from Brough, not sure whether to be pleased or insulted that he had released her immediately.

His own face was turned away from her as he looked up towards the terrace, and so she couldn't see his expression nor guess what he was thinking until he said coldly to her, 'You're a very popular woman. First Julian and now Harry—but you'll forgive me, I know, if I decline to join the queue; enticing though what you have to offer undoubtedly is, I'm afraid my tastes run to a woman less practised and more genuine...'

Before Kelly could answer him he had gone, plunging past her into the darkness of the garden.

Shakily she turned towards the steps.

'Thank goodness I've found you,' Harry told her as he saw her. 'Dee would have had my guts for garters if I'd let anything happen to you. I'm under strict instructions to take care of you...' He started to frown, and then told her a little uncomfortably, 'It's none of my business, I know, and Dee's not told me what's going on, but Cox isn't a man I'd want any sister of mine to get involved with, and...'

'You're right,' Kelly agreed in gentle warning. 'It *isn't* any of your business, Harry.'

When they returned to their table they were just in

time to see Brough leaving; giving Harry and Kelly a curt nod, he ignored Eve's protests that it was too early for him to leave.

'I've got a meeting at nine in the morning,' Kelly heard him telling his sister.

'Oh, but you haven't forgotten that you promised to talk with Julian? He has something special to ask you, and there's his new venture, too,' Eve reminded her brother anxiously.

Immediately Kelly's ears pricked up. If Julian was looking for someone to finance a new business venture then Dee would certainly want to know about it. But as though he had somehow sensed her curiosity Brough touched his sister lightly on the arm and told her, 'I'm sure that Harry and Kelly aren't interested in our private family affairs. Cox…' He nodded briefly in Julian's direction before telling him, 'I'll arrange for a taxi to collect Eve—if I were you I'd leave your car behind and organise one for yourself.'

Was she imagining it or had he actually emphasised the word 'private', underlining its significance by giving her a cool, distancing look as he did so?

Whatever the case, Kelly could feel her face starting to burn slightly.

There was no point in her trying to deceive herself. From his demeanour towards his sister, she suspected that he was normally a man who regarded her sex with respect and genuine appreciation, even if at times he did allow his natural male instinct to protect anyone whom he might consider to be vulnerable to surface through his otherwise very politically correct manners. But where she was concerned he had displayed the kind of behaviour that was very far from treating her with respect. That kiss they had exchanged, which for her had been an act of heart-shakingly emotional and physical sensual significance, a complete one-off in her life and totally different from anything she had done or experienced before, had for him simply been an endorsement of the fact that her deliberately flirtatious behaviour with Julian meant that she was open to all manner of unpleasant male behaviour.

The kiss, which had seemed so deeply meaningful and intimate to her, had quite obviously for him merely been a reinforcement of his contempt for her, an emotionally barren male reaction to what he must have seen as some kind of casual, careless open invitation from her.

This kind of situation was so alien to her that Kelly had no knowledge of how to deal with it, and her instinctive desire to confront him and challenge his attitude towards her was further complicated and hampered by the role she was having to play.

Anyway, she decided firmly half an hour later as Harry was driving her home, why was she bothering wasting so much time worrying about what Brough Frobisher may or may not think about her? Why indeed! Julian, though, certainly seemed to have taken the bait, as Dee had planned he would. Kelly gave a small shudder of disgust—the heel.

She grimaced a little, remembering the open interest Julian had shown in the pearl earrings and solitaire ring she had been wearing—an inspired addition to her outfit on her own part; unlike her couture gown and earrings, the ring was anything but genuine, but Julian had certainly been taken in by it—just as his unworldly naive victims had been taken in by him. Dee was right—it was time someone turned the tables on him—but, much as she wanted to help her friend, Kelly had to admit to wishing there might be some other way she could do so.

'You, Kelly are suddenly going to become an extremely rich young woman,' Dee had told her. 'All you have to do is let him believe that you're prepared to commit yourself and, more importantly, your future to him. His own ego and his greed will do the rest.'

Kelly hoped that she was right, because there was certainly no way she was going to be able to give Julian any physical, sexual confirmation of her supposed desire for him. No way at all!

CHAPTER FOUR

KELLY looked up as she heard the shop doorbell go. She was expecting Dee. They had spoken on the phone earlier when Dee had announced that she intended to come round to collect the ballgown accessories which had, in fact, been hired from an exclusive dress shop and to discuss what had happened at the ball.

Kelly had had a pleasingly busy morning with several customers. She hoped that Beth *was* going to be able to source a supplier of high-quality glass in the Czech Republic as this morning alone she had promised three potentially interested customers that they were hopefully going to be able to provide them with the sets of stemware they wanted.

'Something different...something pretty...something not too expensive...' had been the heartfelt pleas of their potential customers. Fingers crossed that if Beth's quest was successful they would be able to meet all three requirements.

'Right,' Dee commanded briskly as she walked up to the counter. 'How did the ball go? Tell me everything...'

'Julian was there with his new girlfriend,' Kelly began, pausing before she added quietly, 'I felt so sorry for her, Dee. She's plainly very much in love with him and so young and naive... I hate the thought of doing anything that might hurt her...'

'She'll be hurt much, much more if Julian succeeds in persuading her to marry him, which he's going to go all out to do. His finances are in a complete mess and getting worse by the day. He's desperately in need of money. She's quite wealthy in her own right and then, when you add on the financial benefits which could accrue to him through her brother... But from what Harry has told me Julian was making a very definite play for you...'

'Yes, he was,' Kelly agreed, tracing an abstract design with the tip of her finger on the polished glass counter before saying hesitantly, 'Dee, I'm not sure if I can go on with what we planned. I don't like Julian, and, whilst I like even less what he's done to Beth and what he's doing to Eve Frobisher, I...'

'Would it help if I gave you my solemn promise that on no account and on no occasion would I *ever* allow a situation to arise where you would have to be on your own with him?' Dee asked her.

Kelly stared at her. How on earth had Dee guessed what was troubling her?

'You're quite right,' Dee told her, answering the question Kelly still had to ask. 'I wouldn't want to be on my own with him either, especially if I thought that there was any risk that he might guess what we're up to... Harry is quite aggrieved with me, you know,' she added with a chuckle. 'He not only feels that as your friend and landlady I ought to put you wise to Julian's real character, he also shares your concern on behalf of Eve Frobisher.

'In fact,' she told Kelly ruefully, 'I'm afraid he's rather taken me to task over the whole thing.'

'Does he now know what we're doing, then?' Kelly asked her in some surprise. Instinctively she had felt that Dee was a woman who exercised her own judgement, made her own decisions and played her cards very close to her chest.

'Not entirely,' Dee admitted, confirming Kelly's private thoughts. 'Harry is a sweetie, as solid and dependable as they come. He wouldn't recognise a lie if he met one walking down the street; subterfuge and everything that goes with it is very much alien territory to him, which does have its advantages, of course. He's wonderful potential husband and father material...' She cocked a thoughtful eye at Kelly. 'He's comfortably off, and I know for a fact that his mother is dying for him to settle down and produce children. If you were interested...'

'He's a honey,' Kelly told her hastily, 'but not, I'm afraid, my type.'

Nor, she suspected, was she his, but she rather thought she knew someone who might be. She hadn't missed the anxious and protective looks Harry had been giving Eve over dinner the previous night.

'Mmm... Pity... Look, I've got to dash,' Dee told her. 'When Julian rings you—which he will—I want to know about it...'

'Dee,' Kelly said, but it was too late; the other woman was already heading for the door, ignoring her half-panicky protests.

What was Dee saying? Julian wouldn't ring her. He wouldn't dare. Flirting with her last night was one thing, but...

In her heart of hearts Kelly knew that despite her desire to do the right thing by Beth and the rest of her sex she was secretly reluctant to have anything more to do with Julian. Not because she feared him. She didn't. No. Contempt, dislike, anger...those were the emotions he aroused within her.

Admit it, she told herself sternly ten minutes later as she locked the shop and disappeared into the small back room to have her lunch, 'you just hate the thought of anyone thinking you could possibly be attracted to him. *Anyone*…or a specific someone…a *very* specific someone.

Pushing aside her half-eaten sandwich, Kelly started to frown. Don't start that again, she warned herself. He's not much better than Julian… Look at the way he treated you. Kissing you like that.

Kissing her… Abruptly she sat down, her insides starting to melt and then ache.

Watch it, she warned herself, deriding herself fiercely. It isn't just your insides he's turning to mush, it's your brain as well.

Her frown deepened as she heard someone ringing the shop doorbell. Couldn't they read? They were closed. The ringing persisted. Irritably Kelly got up. There was no way she could finish her lunch with that row going on.

Opening the communicating door, she marched into the shop and then stopped abruptly as she saw Brough Frobisher standing on the other side of the plate-glass window.

Her hand went to her throat in an instinctive gesture of shock as she breathed in disbelief, 'You.'

Shakily she went to unlock the shop door. Brough was frowning as he stepped inside.

'I'm looking for Kay Harris,' he told her abruptly. The sense of shock that hit her was so strong that for a moment Kelly was unable to reply.

'She does work here, doesn't she?' Brough was demanding curtly, looking at her, Kelly realised, as though he doubted her ability to answer him competently.

'Yes. Yes, she does… I do… It's Kelly, not Kay,' Kelly corrected him shakily. 'K is just my initial.'

'You!'

Sensing his reluctance to believe her, Kelly drew herself up to her full height and told him in her most businesslike voice, 'My partner and I run this shop.'

'You paint china?' His disbelief was palpable and insulting.

Kelly could feel her temper starting to ignite. There were many things she was not, and she had her fair share of human faults and frailties, but there was one thing that she was sure of and that was that she was extremely good at her chosen work—and that wasn't merely her own opinion.

'Yes, I do. Perhaps you'd like to see my credentials?' she suggested bitingly.

'I thought I just did—last night.' The long, slow, arrogantly male look he gave her made her face burn and her temper heat to simmering point.

'What is it exactly that you want?' she demanded angrily, adding before she could stop herself, 'If it's simply because you're some sort of weirdo who gets off on insulting women, I should have thought your behaviour towards me last night would have more than satisfied you.'

Kelly knew that she had overstepped the mark. She could hardly believe what she had just heard herself say, but it was too late to withdraw her remarks. Retaliation couldn't be long in coming, she recognised, and she was right.

'If you're referring to the fact that I kissed you...' he began silkily, and then paused whilst he looked straight into her eyes. 'Allow me to say that you have a rather...unusual...way of expressing your...displeasure...'

He didn't say anything more—he didn't need to, Kelly

acknowledged; the expression in his eyes and the tone of his voice along with the masterly understatement of his silky words was more than enough to leave her covered in confusion and angry, self-inflicted humiliation.

'I… You… It was a mistake,' was all she could think of to say.

'Oh, yes,' he agreed dulcetly. 'It certainly was. Now, I'm afraid that I am rather short of time. I have a commission I would like to discuss with you.'

Kelly blinked. All that and he *still* wanted to talk business with her.

Her thoughts must have shown in her face because he explained gently, 'You're my last resort. You have, or so I am told, a very particular and rare skill. It will soon be my grandmother's eightieth birthday. She has a Rockingham-style teaset, a much cherished family heirloom, but some pieces are missing, broken many years ago. The set has no particular material value; its value to her is in the fact that it was a wedding gift from her grandparents. I have managed to find out that Hartwell China bought out the original manufacturers many, many years ago and, whilst they still produce china in the same shape, they no longer produce the same pattern.

'To have one of their own artists copy such an intricate floral design would, they say, prove far too costly— the work would have to be done by one of the top workers, which would mean taking him or her off work they already have in hand. They recommended that I got in touch with you. Apparently there is no one else they would allow, never mind recommend, to do such work.'

'I…I worked for them whilst I was at university,' Kelly explained huskily. 'That was when I discovered that I had some talent for…for china-painting. I would have to see the design... It wouldn't be easy...or cheap...' she warned him.

Against her will she had been touched by the story he had told her, but *she* knew, even if he didn't, just how intricate and time-consuming the kind of work he was describing could be.

'I've managed to cadge one of the tea plates from Nan, and Hartwell have very kindly said that I can use their archive records.'

'Do you have the plate with you?' Kelly asked him.

He shook his head, unexpectedly looking oddly boyish as he admitted, 'I'm terrified of breaking it. I've got it at home. I was wondering if it would be possible for you to call there to see it.'

Kelly wanted to refuse, but her professional pride and curiosity proved too strong for her.

'I could,' she agreed cautiously, 'but it would have to be when the shop is closed. My partner, Beth, is away at the moment.'

'Could you manage this evening?'

'I...'

'I don't have very much time left. Nan's birthday isn't very far away,' he told her.

Kelly sighed. There was no reason why she shouldn't look at the plate this evening.

'I suppose so,' she agreed reluctantly. 'Where do you live? I—' She broke off as the phone began to ring, automatically going to answer it, saying, 'Excuse me a moment...' as she picked up the receiver.

'Hi, Kelly, it's Julian. How are you, you delicious, hot, sexy thing...?'

Kelly almost dropped the receiver as Julian's loud voice seemed to fill the shop. Her face burning with embarrassment, she turned her back on Brough even though she knew that he could well have heard what Julian had said.

'Julian. I...I'm busy...' she protested. 'I...'

'I understand, babe. What you and I have to say to one another needs to be said in private, right?' Julian responded. 'God, but you turned me on last night, doll... I can't wait for us to get together...'

'Julian.' Kelly closed her eyes, as revolted by Julian's conversation as she was by his person. 'Julian, please—' she began. But he wouldn't let her finish, interrupting her to say thickly, 'I'll ring you later at the flat. I've still got the number...'

He had hung up before Kelly could object or protest, leaving her pink cheeked both with anger and chagrin— anger because of Julian's assumption that she, or any other woman for that matter, would be willing to see him when he was supposedly already involved with someone else, and chagrin because Brough could have overheard some of the conversation.

It was to be expected, of course, that he wouldn't let the matter go without comment, especially when the girl whom Julian was supposed to be on the point of becoming engaged to was his own sister.

'I appreciate that custom has it that there's supposedly safety in numbers, but don't you think you could be interpreting its validity just a little too generously?' he asked her smoothly.

'Julian is an old friend,' Kelly reminded him.

The look he gave her could have stopped Linford Christie in his tracks, Kelly felt sure.

'Really? Then I feel extremely sorry for you, not only in your unfortunate choice of *friends* but your misplaced and, no doubt, regularly abused loyalty.'

'Julian is dating your sister,' Kelly felt compelled to remind him defensively.

He had turned to walk towards the door, but now, abruptly, he stopped and turned back to Kelly, and said quietly but with grim force, 'Yes, he is, isn't he?' And then, almost without pausing, he added coolly, 'Shall we say eight tonight? This is the address...'

Kelly was still looking bemusedly at the business card he had placed down on the counter as he closed the shop door behind him.

Why on earth hadn't she said something, objected to his high-handed assumption that she would not merely be free this evening but that, additionally, she would fall in with his plans, agree to his request, especially in view of the way he had spoken to her?

Reluctantly she picked up the card. Kelly had a vague idea where the house was since it was on the same road as a customer who had ordered a special commission from her.

Ten minutes before she was due to re-open the shop, the phone rang again. This time the caller was Beth, ringing from Prague.

'Hi... How are things going?' Kelly asked her eagerly.

'Not too bad, in fact really quite promisingly. I've been given several contact numbers, and I'm due to drive out of the city tomorrow to visit a crystal factory.'

'And you're managing okay, despite the language barrier?' Kelly asked her. This had been one of Beth's main concerns about her trip and Kelly was anxious to know how her friend was coping.

'Oh, I've got an interpreter,' Beth told her.

Kelly frowned. The offhand tone of Beth's voice was both unfamiliar and slightly worrying.

'And she's helping you, visiting factories with you...?'

'*She* is a he,' Beth told her shortly. 'And as for *helping* me...' There was a small pause. 'Honestly, Kelly, men. I'm totally off all of them. Just because a person has a fancy degree and a whole string of letters after his name, that does *not* give him the right to try to tell *me* what to do. And as for trying to force me to visit factories that *he's* chosen, with tales of theft and gypsies—'

'Beth.' Kelly interrupted her in bewilderment. 'I'm sorry, but I don't understand.'

'Oh, it's all right, I'm just letting off steam. It's Alex, the interpreter. He's half-English, as it turns out, and his grandparents left Prague for political asylum in the west when his mother was a child. Alex returned after the revolution to search for his family and he's stayed on here.'

'Sounds like he's been confiding rather a lot of personal history to you for someone you don't get on with,' Kelly told her wryly.

'Oh, he tells me what he wants me to know. He's insisting that I visit a glass factory run by his cousins, but I'm not inclined to go. He obviously has a vested interest in anything I might buy. I've managed to track down somewhere that produces this most wonderful design I've seen, and he's acting all high and mighty and trying to tell me that it's all a con and that the stallholder saw me coming a mile off. He says there *isn't* any factory where they've told me to go and the glass I wanted to buy couldn't have been genuine. He says it's a well-known ploy to get hold of foreign currency that is often worked against naive people like me...

'Oh, but Kelly, you should have seen this glass. It was wonderful, pure Venetian baroque, you know the kind of thing, and it would lend itself beautifully to being gilded for the Christmas market. I even thought that if the price was reasonable enough we could commission some special sets, hand-painted and gilded for special celebrations—weddings, anniversaries...you know the kind of thing...'

Kelly laughed as she listened to her friend's excited enthusiasm. It was wonderful to hear that note back in Beth's voice again, and even more wonderful that she hadn't even asked once about Julian Cox.

'Anyway,' Beth was continuing determinedly, 'somehow I'm going out to this factory by myself. I'm planning to give my guide, and for that you can read jailer, the slip. It's obvious what he's up to,' she told Kelly scornfully. 'He just wants to secure our business for his cousins. He claims that their factory could probably reproduce the glass if they had a copy of it...'

'Mmm... Well, if that's the case, it might be worthwhile sketching the glass and seeing if they *can* reproduce it.'

'Never,' Beth asserted fiercely. 'There's no way I'm going to have Alex dictating to me... No. I've seen the glass I want and I know where to get it, and I'm determined to get an exclusive supply of it and at the right price. After all, if we did commission Alex's cousins, what's to stop them selling our design elsewhere, putting up the price to us because they know we want it? Look, I must go; Alex is picking me up in half an hour. He's insisting on making me walk over the Charles Bridge, and since it's raining today he says it should be relatively free of other tourists.'

'Sounds fun,' Kelly teased her, smiling as she said goodbye and hung up. The others would be so pleased to hear that Beth seemed to be getting over Julian Cox.

CHAPTER FIVE

AS HE let himself into the hallway of their rented house and blinked at the teeth-jarring hard yellow paint of the room, Brough reflected that he would be glad when they could finally move into the large Georgian farmhouse he had bought several miles outside the town and which was presently undergoing some much needed renovation work. It had been empty for three years before Brough had managed to persuade the trustees of the estate of the late owner that there was no way anyone was ever going to pay the exorbitant price they were asking for it.

'If they don't sell it soon, they'll be lucky to have anything there worth selling,' he had told the agent crisply. 'It's already been empty and unheated for three winters, and if the government gives the go-ahead for the new bypass the area will be swarming with protestors just looking for an empty house to take over and make themselves comfortable in.'

Buying the house, though, had simply been the beginning of a whole spate of difficult negotiations. The property was listed, and every detail of his planning applications had to be scanned by what had felt like a never-ending chain of committees, but now at last the approved builder had started work on the property, and, with any luck, he should be able to move into it within the year, the builder had assured him cheerfully on his last site inspection.

For now, he would have to live with the last owner

of his present house's headache-inducing choice of colours.

'Brough, is that you?'

He grimaced wryly as Eve came rushing into the hallway, her face pink with excitement as she told him breathlessly, 'Guess what? Julian rang; he's going to be free this evening after all, so he's taking me out to dinner. Oh, Brough, I was so afraid he was going to be angry with me when you insisted that you couldn't help him with his new venture.'

As he listened to her Brough could feel himself starting to grind his teeth. There was no point in wishing that his sister had a more worldly and less naive outlook, nor in blaming his grandmother and the old-fashioned girls' school she had insisted he send her to for the part they had played in her upbringing. He might just as well blame their parents for dying—and himself for not being able to take on the full responsibility for bringing her up without his grandmother's help.

He knew how upset his grandmother would be if she knew how ill-prepared the select, protective girls' school she had chosen so carefully for her had left Eve for the modern world, and some day in the not too distant future Brough was afraid that his sister was going to have her eyes opened to reality in a way that was going to hurt her very badly.

As he'd thought a number of times before, there was no point in him trying to warn Eve about Julian Cox. She had a surprisingly strong, stubborn streak to her make-up, and was very sensitive about both her own independence and her judgement. To imply that Julian was deceiving her, that she was totally and completely wrong about him in every single way, was almost guaranteed to send her running into his arms, and not away from them, which would have been bad enough if what she stood to lose from such an event was her emotional and physical innocence—more than bad enough. But Eve stood to inherit a very sizeable sum of money from their parents' estate when she reached her twenty-fifth birthday, and Brough was convinced that Julian Cox would have no compunction whatsoever about marrying her simply for that reason alone.

Brough had had Julian's financial affairs thoroughly investigated. To describe them as in total disarray and bordering on the legally fraudulent was no exaggeration, nor was his emotional history any less murky. But, of course, Eve wouldn't hear a word against him. She considered herself to be in love.

'Oh, I'm so pleased. He was awfully upset this morning after you told him you really couldn't help him... That was mean of you,' she reproached Brough.

'On the contrary, it was simply good business sense,' Brough told her dryly. 'I know how you feel about him, Eve but...'

'Oh, Brough, please don't start lecturing me,' she begged him. 'Just because you don't want to fall in love...because you don't have someone to share your life with...someone special...that doesn't mean... I love him, Brough,' she said simply.

Brough sighed as she went upstairs. He wished he could find some way to protect her from the ultimate inevitability of having her heart broken, but he suspected that even if he were to confront her with incontrovertible evidence of Cox's real nature she would simply close her eyes to it.

Women! There was no way of understanding how their minds and, even more, their emotions worked. Look at Kelly. A bright, intelligent, beautiful young woman who was apparently as oblivious to Cox's faults as his own sister. Not that he thought that Kelly's other choice of male was any better—but for very different reasons. Harry was quite obviously an extremely estimable young man, the kind of man whom he would have been only too pleased to see dating his *sister*, but, as a partner for a woman of Kelly's obviously feisty and quicksilver personality, surely a totally wrong choice. She needed a man who could match the quickness of her brain...who could appreciate the intelligence and artistry of her work...who could share the passion that he could sense ran so strongly through her at the very deepest level of her personality... A man who...

Abruptly he caught himself up.

Nothing he had experienced in his admittedly brief contact with Kelly had indicated that she had the kind of insecure, needy personality that would make her a natural victim for a man like Cox.

Eve, on the other hand, if he was honest, desperately needed to feel loved and secure, to have a partner who would incorporate into their adult relationship the kind of protective, emotional padding she had missed from the loss of their father and experienced in a different way at school. Eve needed a man who would treat her gently, a man with whom she could have the kind of relationship which he privately would find too unequal. The woman he loved would have to be his equal, his true partner in every aspect of their lives. There would have to be complete and total honesty and commitment between them, a deep, inner knowledge that they would be there for one another through their whole lives—he too had suffered from their parents' death, he acknowledged wryly.

And Eve was wrong about him not wanting to fall in

love…to marry. At the end of his present decade lay the watershed birthday of forty, comfortably in the distance as yet, but still there on the horizon. When he thought of himself as forty, it was not particularly pleasant to visualise himself still alone, uncommitted…childless… But the woman he married, the woman he loved…

Unbidden, the memory of how Kelly's lips had felt beneath his flooded his body, sharply reminding him that if a male's sexual responses were at their fastest and peak in his teens, then they could still react with a pretty forceful and demanding potent speed in his thirties—disconcertingly so.

The dichotomy he had sensed within Kelly at the ball which had so intrigued him had turned to a more personal sense of irritation this afternoon. Did she really think he was so lacking in intelligence…in awareness…that he couldn't see how alien to her personality her relationship with Julian was? What the hell was it about the man that led a woman like her to…? It was almost as though he held some kind of compulsive attraction for her or had some kind of hold over her.

In another age it might almost have been said that he had cast some kind of spell over her—as she was beginning to do over him?

Kelly paused in the act of picking up her keys. In the close confines of the flat's small entrance hall she could smell the scent of her own perfume. Defensively she told herself that wearing it was simply second nature to her and meant nothing, had no dark, deep, psychological significance, that the fact that she was wearing it to, and for, a meeting with Brough Frobisher meant absolutely nothing at all.

She wasn't a woman who was overly fond of striking

make-up, nor strictly styled hair, but she did like the femininity of wearing her own special signature scent, even if normally she wore it in conjunction with jeans and a casual top.

Tonight, though, those jeans had been exchanged for a well-cut trouser suit—not for any other reason than the fact that wearing it automatically made her feel more businesslike. And that was, after all, exactly what this evening's meeting was all about—business. And as for that small spurt of sweet, sharp excitement she could feel dancing over her vulnerable nerve-endings, well, that was nothing more than the arousal of her professional curiosity.

Hartwell china always evoked special memories for her. It had been the Hartwell china she had seen on a visit to a stately home as a girl which had first awoken her interest in the design and manufacture of porcelain, and it had been the Hartwell factory where she had first had her actual hands-on experience of working on the physical aspect of copying the designer's artistry onto the china itself. And so it was only natural that she should feel this surge of excitement at the thought of seeing a piece which sounded as though it was extremely rare.

It didn't take her very long to drive to the address Brough had given her. Rye-on-Averton was only a relatively small and compact town, virtually untouched by any effects of the Industrial Revolution and still surrounded by the farmland which had surrounded it way, way back in the Middle Ages.

Parking her own car and getting out, Kelly carefully skirted the expensive gleaming Mercedes saloon car parked in the drive and climbed the three steps which led to the front door. Brough opened it for her virtually as soon as she rang the bell.

Unlike her, he was unexpectedly casually dressed in jeans and a soft cotton checked shirt.

The jeans, Kelly noticed as she responded to his non-verbal invitation to come into the house, somehow or other emphasised the lean length of his legs and the powerful strength of his thigh muscles.

As a part of her studies at university she had, for a term, attended a series of lectures and drawing classes on the human body, and whilst there had been required to sketch nudes, both male and female, but that experience was still no protection against either the images which inexplicably filled her thoughts or the guilty burn of colour which accompanied them.

What on earth was she doing, mentally envisaging Brough posing, modelling for a classical Greek statue? That kind of behaviour, those kinds of thoughts, simply were not her.

'It's this way,' Brough informed her, the cool, clipped sound of his voice breaking into the dangerous heat of her thoughts as he indicated one of the doorways off the hall.

The yellow paint in which the hallway was decorated made Kelly do a slight double-take, a fact which Brough obviously noticed because he commented dryly, 'Bilious, isn't it? Unfortunately its shock effect doesn't lessen with time.'

'You could always redecorate,' Kelly pointed out austerely, refusing to allow herself to feel any sympathy with him, even in the unfortunate colour of his walls.

'Not really. This house is only rented. I'm only living here until the one I've bought has been renovated.'

'Oh, so you've moved into the area permanently, then?'

Kelly berated herself furiously as the question slipped out, her curiosity getting the better of her, but to her relief Brough made totally the wrong connection between her question and its motivation as he responded even more dryly, 'Yes, we have, so I'm afraid you can't look to our removal from town as an easy way of removing my sister from your lover's life.'

'It isn't necessary for me to do any such thing,' Kelly denied furiously through gritted teeth, momentarily forgetting her allotted role.

'Eve believes he intends to marry her. How do you feel about that?' he challenged her.

'How do you feel about it?' Kelly sidetracked.

'He's a liar and a cheat and most probably guilty of financial fraud as well,' Brough told her bitingly. 'How the hell do you think I feel about it?'

'She's *your* sister.'

'Strange,' he continued softly, 'you don't look particularly surprised—or shocked. Perhaps you *like* the idea of having a married lover, especially one whose wife is both extremely rich and extremely in love.'

'No. That's not...'

Immediately she realised what she was saying, Kelly stopped.

'That's not what?' Brough goaded her. 'Not what you want? He's *your* lover...'

'And Eve is *your* sister,' Kelly pointed out again quickly. 'My relationship with Julian is no one's business other than our own. If you dislike him so much, *disapprove* of him so much, why haven't you told Eve so?'

'She's too much in love to listen to me or to anyone

else. What *is* it you see in him? What possible attraction can he have for any woman when he…?'

'Why don't you ask Eve?' Kelly suggested.

Ridiculously, dangerously, she was actually starting to feel sorry for him. It was plain how worried he was about his sister, and with good reason, and it was equally plain that he felt helpless to do anything to alter the situation. Even so, she couldn't resist punishing him just a little, both for what he thought about her and what he had said…and done…

'It's obviously hard for a man to see just what it is about Julian that appeals to our sex. Perhaps you feel jealous of him.'

'Jealous…? Look, just because last night I *kissed* you, that doesn't mean—'

'I mean jealous because Eve loves him,' Kelly interrupted him shakily.

'You wanted me to look at this plate,' she reminded him, anxious to return their conversation to a much more businesslike footing.

'Yes. It's in here,' he told her, ushering her into a large, high-ceilinged room which was painted a particularly unpleasant shade of dull green.

'Hideous, isn't it?' he agreed, correctly interpreting her thoughts. 'The owner must be colour blind—or worse. You should see the bedrooms; the one I'm occupying is painted a particularly repulsive shade of puce.'

'Puce…? I don't believe you,' Kelly protested. 'No one would paint a bedroom that colour.'

'If you want to see for yourself I'll show you afterwards…' Brough started to say, and then stopped to study Kelly's bright pink face with interest.

'Now there's an interesting conundrum,' he mused

sardonically. 'Why should a woman who openly admits that she is sleeping with another woman's boyfriend blush at the mere mention of a completely altruistic visit to another man's bedroom? It *was* my bedroom I was suggesting you view,' he added gently, 'not my bed...'

'I was *not* blushing,' Kelly protested. 'It's just...it's just...it's very warm in here...'

'Is it?' Brough asked, adding, 'Then what, may I ask, are these?'

Before she could stop him he was running a hard fingertip down the full length of her bare arm, right over the rash of goose bumps which had lifted beneath her skin when they'd entered the room's unheated atmosphere. And what made it worse was that the brief and totally sexless stroke of his finger had made the goose bumps even more prominent—and not just her goose bumps, she acknowledged, mortified by the unwanted discovery that her nipples were inexplicably pressing very hard, tightly aroused, against the constraining fabric of her bra.

Instinctively she turned away from him, lifting her arm in what she hoped was a natural and subtle gesture which he wouldn't guess was designed to conceal the evidence of her body's extraordinary behaviour from him.

He had seen it, though, seen it and been both disgusted and angered by it, she recognised, if the look she could see in his eyes was anything to go by.

My God, but she had got it badly if even the mere fact of talking about Cox could arouse her body like that, Brough fumed as Kelly turned her flushed face and aroused breasts out of his eye-line.

It had been bad enough when he had simply wanted to protect and rescue his sister from the man, but now...

'The plate's over here,' he told Kelly curtly.

Silently she followed him, keeping her distance from him as he unlocked the small corner cupboard and removed the plate, but as he walked over to her and she saw it she couldn't resist giving a small cry of pleasure, closing the distance between them so that she could take the plate from him and study it more closely.

'Oh, it's beautiful,' she enthused as she traced the design lovingly with her fingertip. 'Almost Sèvres in style and execution...'

'Yes, that's what they said at the factory. They suspect that the whole set might have been a showpiece set made by a particularly gifted apprentice. Apparently, when they finished their time in apprenticeship the artists were often given the opportunity to do something to act as a showcase for their skills.'

'Yes, I know,' Kelly agreed absently, barely able to take her glance off the plate. 'Oh, it's lovely—so detailed and intricate.'

She stopped and shook her head.

'What's wrong? Don't you think you can copy it?' Brough asked her.

Kelly paused.

'I don't know,' she admitted. 'It's very complex, and the gold leaf work alone would be so expensive in materials... I... Can't Hartwell recommend anyone else to do it for you, someone more experienced?'

Brough gave her a level look.

'According to them there *isn't* anyone more experienced,' he told her quietly.

To her annoyance Kelly knew that she was blushing again.

'I... I... It's very kind of them to say so, but...'

'They also told me that you turned down a very lucrative and secure contract with them to go into business by yourself.'

'I…I like being my own boss,' Kelly told him quietly.

'Even though it doesn't pay you anything like as well as working for them would have done…?'

'Money isn't that important to me,' Kelly admitted after a small pause. There followed a very stiff, very pregnant silence during which Kelly recognised that she had said something wrong, but was not sure what.

'I suppose you don't agree with that kind of outlook at all,' she challenged him when the silence had made her skin start to prickle. 'I expect *you* feel that when a person doesn't exploit their…talents to the best possible financial advantage, then—'

'On the contrary,' Brough interrupted her firmly. '*I* feel extremely sorry for anyone who feels obliged to accept a way of life, a means of living, that doesn't make them happy.'

'But you can't believe that earning money isn't of prime importance to me,' Kelly insisted.

'What I can't believe is that a woman holding the views you've just expressed would in any way consider a man like Julian Cox to be a good partner for her,' Brough corrected her.

'I…I didn't come here to discuss my relationship with Julian,' Kelly told him tautly, handing the plate back to him as she did so, giving it a last lingering look of regret. There was nothing she would have loved more than to copy the design and replace the missing pieces of the teaset, especially under the circumstances Brough had outlined to her. But she couldn't do anything that would bring her into closer contact with him. There was too much risk involved in far too many different ways.

But before she could vocalise her decision, Brough

himself was speaking, telling her coolly, 'We don't have much time left before my grandmother's birthday, so I've arranged for us to visit the factory on Wednesday. They told me when I was there that you'd need to collect the unpainted china from them and get supplies of paint.'

'Wednesday? But it's Monday today; I can't possibly...' Kelly began.

But he was already overruling her, telling her, 'I know what you're going to say and I've asked Eve if she will stand in at the shop for you for the day. She's agreed. And before you say anything you needn't worry—she did a stint at Harvey Nicks during her last year at school.'

'Harvey Nicks?' Kelly exploded, adding pointedly, 'This isn't Knightsbridge...'

'No, it isn't,' he agreed. 'We'll need to get a pretty early start, so if I pick you up at, say, eight I can drop Eve off at the same time.'

'Just a minute,' Kelly objected. 'I haven't agreed that I'm going—'

'What's wrong? Are you afraid that Cox might object to you spending the day with me?'

'This has *nothing* to do with Julian,' Kelly told him angrily.

'Good. So I'll pick you up at eight on Wednesday, then,' Brough repeated cordially as he walked over to the door and held it open for her.

There was no way she was going to be able to make him understand that she wasn't going to Staffordshire with him, Kelly recognised, irritably marching straight past him and heading for the front door, where he caught up with her and commented dulcetly, 'I take it you've decided to accept my word about the colour of my bedroom walls...'

Kelly shot him a fulminating look. 'The colour of your bedroom walls, be they puce, chartreuse or vermilion, is totally and absolutely of no interest to me,' she told him.

'Vermilion,' Brough mused. 'The colour of passion. Interesting that you should suggest it...'

'*Suggest* it? I did no such thing.' Kelly seethed. 'What do you think you're *doing*?' she demanded as, instead of opening the front door, he very gently and totally unexpectedly placed his hands on her upper arms and turned her round.

'I'm going to make you a cup of cocoa before you go home,' he told her, adding suavely, 'It warms the blood and soothes the passions. The Aztecs used to believe it had aphrodisiac powers, as did the Regency bucks. There's no point in you rushing back. Julian is out with Eve.'

'What's that got to do with me? I've got a deskful of paperwork needing attention, and anyway, I *loathe* cocoa,' she told him pettishly.

'A glass of wine perhaps, then,' he suggested.

Kelly started to shake her head, and then for some reason found that she was nodding it slowly instead.

'This way,' he told her, directing her further down the hallway and into another room, which was a cross between an office and a study, comfortably furnished with a couple of deep armchairs and a huge desk which dominated the space in front of the window.

'For Christmas the year before last, Eve rented for me a row of vines in France. The idea is that you get the wine from your own vines and you can, if you wish, take part in some of the preparation of the wine. Surprisingly, it's rather good...'

'So you'll what?' Kelly asked him. 'Buy the vine-yard?'

An unexpected smile tugged at the corners of his mouth.

'Not this particular one,' he admitted. 'But it's certainly an idea. I wouldn't have an objection to a life of viticulture and semi-retirement... Tuscany, perhaps, close to one of those unbelievably visually breathtaking medieval towns...'

'It sounds idyllic,' Kelly responded enviously, without thinking, and then bit her lip, telling him curtly, 'Look, I really can't stay. Paperwork isn't really my strong suit and...'

'I understand,' Brough accepted. His face was in the shadows but there was no mistaking the stiffness in his voice. Quite patently he was angry with her again, Kelly decided, suppressing a soft sigh. So why should she care either what he thought or what he felt? This time, as she headed for the front door, he made no attempt to persuade her to stay, simply opening it for her and formally thanking her for her time.

As he watched her until she was safely inside the car, Brough wondered what on earth had possessed him to reveal that long-held dream of his to her. What possible interest could it be to her, and, more disturbingly, why should he want it to be?

She was an enigma, a puzzle of unfathomable proportions, and he was a fool for even beginning to think what he was thinking about her.

As he went upstairs and switched on the light in his puce-walled bedroom, his glance rested on the neat white line of his bed. He had been lying when he had told her that it was his bedroom he had been inviting her to see and not his bed. Already, with remarkably little effort at all, he could picture her lying there in it, tucked securely beneath its protective sheets as they outlined the warm curves of her body, holding out an invitation which she mirrored as she held out her arms to welcome him.

Eve hadn't had a good night. She and Julian had had an argument, a small altercation which had blown up out of virtually nothing, simply her innocent comment that Kelly was a very attractive and vivacious woman and that she and Julian were obviously very good friends. But Julian had reacted as though she had accused him of some crime, exploding into a rage so intense that he had actually frightened her.

Shocked and in tears, she had run from his flat, ignoring his demands to her to come back as she'd fired the engine of her car, and here she was now, her car parked in the town centre as she walked unhappily along the riverbank, desperately trying to avoid looking at the entwined pairs of lovers enjoying a romantic stroll along the river path.

'Eve… Eve…'

Instinctively, she stopped as she heard the male voice calling her name, her breath catching in her throat as she recognised Harry hurrying towards her.

'I saw you as I walked over the bridge,' Harry told her with a warm beam as he indicated the bridge she had just passed, his smile fading as he saw her miserable expression. 'What is it? What's wrong?'

'Nothing,' Eve fibbed, but his concern, his sympathy and most of all his sturdy male warmth and reassurance were too much for her already shaky composure, and as she spoke she gave a small hiccuping sob and a tear ran betrayingly down her face.

'It's Cox, isn't it?' Harry guessed, revealing an intuition which would have surprised his relatives, who considered him to be good hearted enough but a trifle lacking in anything requiring mental agility and speed.

'We've had a row,' Eve admitted, immediately adding protectively, 'It was my fault. I...I mentioned Kelly and that made him angry... I shouldn't have brought up the subject. Of course he's entitled to his past and to...'

She stopped as Harry gave a fierce snort of disapproval.

'Of course you're upset,' he comforted her. 'You've every right to be, especially after the way...'

'He was flirting a little with Kelly at the ball,' Eve agreed, guessing what he was going to say. 'But I know that they're old friends and Julian is such an attractive man...'

Harry gave another snort.

'Oh, I know that you probably don't like him. After all, Kelly is your girlfriend.'

'No, she isn't,' Harry told her promptly. 'I don't have a girlfriend...haven't ever really wanted one until... I escorted Kelly because my cousin asked me to...'

'Oh, I see. So you aren't actually going out with Kelly, then?' Eve asked him ingenuously.

Harry shook his head. 'Nice girl but not my type,' he told her.

Inexplicably, as they walked, Eve discovered that she had moved so close to Harry that when they had to pass another couple it seemed the most natural thing in the world for him to shield her protectively by placing his arm around her.

It was very pleasant to be treated as though she was so fragile, so vulnerable and valuable, Eve acknowledged. It made her feel very safe and very protected...

It made her feel happy. Nothing like as happy as she was with Julian, of course, she decided loyally as Harry gently drew her into the protection of a small grove of trees just off the river path.

'Now look,' he told her firmly, 'you mustn't let Cox upset you. He's damn lucky to have a lovely girl like you…damn lucky…'

'Oh, Harry, *I'm* the one who's lucky,' Eve corrected him. 'I'm just plain and ordinary, but Julian…'

'You're no such thing' Harry contradicted her immediately. 'You're beautiful, Eve,' he told her huskily as he looked at her mouth. 'Thought so the moment I saw you…'

An odd quiver of sensation ran right through her body as she recognised the way Harry was looking at her mouth. She might be naive, as she was constantly being told, but she wasn't *that* naive. She was woman enough to know when a man wanted her all right…and when one didn't.

Julian hadn't wanted her tonight. He had pushed her away when she had tried to snuggle into his arms.

'Harry,' she whispered huskily.

'Don't look at me like that, Eve,' he groaned, adding gruffly, 'I want to kiss you so damn much… In fact, I'm *going* to kiss you,' he announced boldly.

Going into Harry's arms was like going home, Eve decided blissfully, all warm and cosy and safe. Happily she turned her face up to his and waited.

She didn't have to wait very long.

His kiss was everything she had known it would be— gentle, reverential, asking, not taking; and it was something more as well, something entirely unexpected and exciting, she recognised as the tiny quivers darting through her body began to grow and gather strength.

'I shouldn't have done that,' Harry told her harshly as he suddenly pushed her away. 'In fact...'

Without saying anything more he turned his back on her and started to walk very quickly away from her.

Feeling as though she had been completely abandoned, Eve stared after him. *Why* had he left her like that? Had he lied to her about not being involved with Kelly? She knew instinctively that Julian had done so when he had told her that Kelly meant absolutely nothing to him. She wasn't completely blind. She had seen the way Julian had been watching Kelly at the ball, but she loved Julian so much...far too much to give him up... Far, far too much to enjoy kissing another man... Hot-cheeked, she pressed her hands to her face. What on earth had she been doing? And why?

It was no wonder, really, that Julian had been so out of sorts and cross, she decided compassionately as she made her way back to her car. It had been a big disappointment for him, poor darling, when Brough had refused to finance his new venture.

She had tried to tell him tonight that she had absolutely no influence at all over Brough's decision, and then he had started to ask her about her own inheritance and she had had to tell him that she couldn't touch a penny of it until she was twenty-five.

'That's four years away,' he had exploded irritably. 'What happens if we get married and you need some money to buy a house?'

If they got married...

'I don't know,' she had confessed, adding brightly, 'Maybe the bank would lend me some money against it... I'd have to check with Brough...'

'No! No, don't do that,' Julian had told her hastily. 'Yes, because when we get married I shall move in here with you, won't I?' she had agreed, blissfully trying to snuggle up against him.

'Yeah...' he had said so unenthusiastically that she had started to frown.

It was then that she had made her first mistake, asking him uncertainly, 'You *do* want to marry me, don't you, Julian? Only I couldn't help noticing at the ball that you seemed awfully interested in Kelly...'

'Kelly's an old friend,' he had told her angrily. 'Not that it's any business of yours...'

Poor darling, of course he was irritable and on edge with all the money worries he was having. It really was too bad of Brough to refuse to help him. Eve's brow creased. She knew, of course, that her brother didn't really like or approve of Julian, but he didn't *know* him the way she did.

CHAPTER SIX

'HI, KELLY, it's Dee.'

Kelly smiled as she recognised their landlady's voice. It was eleven o'clock in the morning and Kelly had just served her third customer and put on the kettle to make herself a cup of coffee.

'Anything to report?' Dee asked her. 'Has Julian been in touch?'

'He rang yesterday,' Kelly told her, 'but I couldn't really talk to him; I had someone here in the shop. You know that Julian is hoping to persuade his girlfriend's brother to finance some new venture he's getting started?'

'*Was* hoping,' Dee corrected her wryly. 'Brough has turned him down.'

How did Dee know that? Kelly wondered curiously.

'Look, we could do with having a meeting,' Dee told her. 'How about lunch tomorrow?'

'Tomorrow? No, I'm afraid I can't,' Kelly told her. 'I'm going to Staffordshire.'

'Staffordshire?' Dee queried sharply. 'On a buying trip? But I thought…'

'No, not that. Actually I'm going with Brough; he's asked me to undertake a private commission for him.'

'And you've agreed?' Dee asked her. 'Be very careful, Kelly. Don't forget his sister is dating Julian and hopes to marry him and he's bound to be extremely suspicious of your role in Julian's life. You haven't told him the truth, have you?' Dee demanded.

'No, of course I haven't,' Kelly reassured her immediately.

'Well, you mustn't. It would ruin everything.'

'I'm not a complete fool, you know, Dee,' Kelly informed her a little irritably. She liked Dee, but sometimes her autocratic attitude irritated her a bit. She wasn't like Beth, who accepted Dee's slight bossiness with placid gentleness even whilst she accepted that the older girl's heart was in the right place and her motives good.

'No, not a complete fool,' Dee agreed dryly, 'but certainly foolish enough to agree to go to Staffordshire with Brough. I understand he's a very attractive man,' she added slyly.

'Not so far as I'm concerned,' Kelly responded immediately, 'but the china he wants me to copy certainly is and, not only that, it's extremely rare and may even be unique. It's a wonderful opportunity, Dee,' she added, warming to her theme, her enthusiasm for the project colouring her voice. 'An almost once-in-a-lifetime chance to work on something very different and very special.

'Oh, Beth rang, by the way,' Kelly informed Dee. 'She's having problems with her interpreter, apparently, but she never said a word about Julian, thank goodness.'

'That *is* good news,' Dee agreed.

'I do feel worried for Eve Frobisher,' Kelly told her.

'You must concentrate on the business in hand,' Dee advised her. 'Eve Frobisher has her brother to protect her interests. Has he said anything about Julian to you, by the way?'

'He's certainly made it plain that he doesn't approve of my relationship with him,' Kelly informed her.

'Mmm... You know, I've been thinking... It could

work to our advantage if you let him think that he might be able to persuade you to have second thoughts about Julian. Men love that—feeling that they're taking charge, doling out advice to some poor, helpless little female. It feeds their egos, and it wouldn't do any harm to get Brough Frobisher on our side.'

'He isn't going to fall for any "helpless little me' act from me, Dee,' Kelly informed her.

'You don't know until you try it,' Dee told her persuasively. 'There's no saying what helpful information we could pick up about Julian's business affairs via him if he—'

'I *don't* know, because there's no way I am going to try it.' Kelly cut across her comment swiftly. 'Tricking Julian into believing I find him attractive is one thing, lying to Brough is quite another...'

'It is? Why?' Dee asked her interestedly.

'Because I don't like lying to anyone,' Kelly told her sharply. 'The only reason I've agreed to deceive Julian is because of what he did to Beth and to stop him from doing it to anyone else. Persuading Brough to believe that I'm some kind of helpless little creature who needs protecting and rescuing from her own emotions, who can't take responsibility for her own life or her own actions, is just so gross that there's no way I would even contemplate it. Besides, he wouldn't believe me. He'd see through what I was trying to do immediately.'

'He knows you that well after spending...how long...a few hours or so with you, does he?' Dee mused. 'Amazing...'

'He believes that I'm intent on trying to take Julian away from his sister. Let's just leave it at that whilst we're ahead of the game, shall we?' Kelly told her curtly, ignoring her gentle jibe.

'Okay,' Dee soothed her, adding, 'Look, I need to have a word with Anna about her making contact with Julian to offer to lend him the money he needs for this new venture. Now that Brough has turned him down he's going to be too urgently in need of financial backing to question Anna's motivation too deeply, which suits us very nicely. Brough has unwittingly done us a very big favour in turning Julian down.'

'I'm sure he'd be delighted to hear that,' Kelly told her *sotto voce*.

'Oh, by the way, Harry sends his best love,' Dee told her teasingly. Kelly grimaced into the receiver.

'He does?' she questioned, unable to resist the temptation to tell Dee dryly, 'That's odd; he seemed far more interested in Eve at the ball than he was in me. Now there's a match. The pair of them are so well suited they might have been made for one another.'

'Eve loves Julian,' Dee pointed out to her.

'No, what she loves is the man she believes that Julian is,' Kelly corrected her soberly. 'Poor girl, he's going to break her heart.'

'Well, if you're right, Harry will be more than willing to help her to mend it,' Dee told her practically. 'Remember, Kelly, you've got to convince Julian that you want him; that way when you drop him as publicly as he dropped Beth he'll never even guess what's going to happen until it does and...'

'I'm not sure that he'll leave Eve for me,' Kelly warned her. 'Eve believes that he's going to marry her...'

'So did Beth and look what happened to her,' Dee pointed out. 'He's going to be furious when he finds out how we've tricked him, furious and totally and completely humiliated,' she said cheerfully. 'And it couldn't happen to a more deserving man.'

'You really hate him, don't you?' Kelly recognised.

'Yes. I really hate him,' Dee agreed, and she put the receiver down. Kelly thought she heard her saying, But nowhere near as much as I hate myself, but she couldn't be sure, and anyway it was too late to question Dee any further since she had hung up.

Wednesday morning came round too soon. Kelly was awake early—too early, she decided as she watched the sun rise.

It still wasn't too late to refuse to go to Staffordshire but what excuse could she realistically give?

Impossible to tell Brough the truth—that she was afraid of going with him, afraid of what she might say, of what he might guess...of what she might feel... But if she didn't go...

Julian had rung her again last night. Reluctantly she had agreed to meet him for a drink at a local wine bar this evening.

'Julian, you're dating someone else,' she had reminded him coldly, 'and so am I...'

'Harry,' he had scoffed. 'He's no match, no man for a woman like you, Kelly.'

'And I suppose that you are,' she had taunted him, holding her breath at the recklessness of what she was doing.

'Try me,' he had told her, sniggering suggestively. 'I promise you, you won't be disappointed.'

Kelly had been glad that the telephone meant he couldn't see the shudder of revulsion she gave.

'You and I are two of a kind, Kelly,' he had told her thickly. 'We take what we want from life. We're both adventurers, exciting…passionate… I knew that the first time I saw you. I knew then how good we'd be together…'

'When you were dating Beth, you mean,' Kelly had reminded him coldly.

'Beth is history,' he'd told her dismissively. 'But you and I…you and I are *now*, Kelly…'

'You and I are *nothing*,' she had told him.

'Tomorrow night,' Julian had countered. 'Be there, Kelly… You know you want me and I sure as hell want you…'

Want him? Completely revolted both by his conversation and his tone of voice, Kelly had replaced the receiver.

She could just imagine what Brough would have to say.

Brough.

Now why on earth was she thinking about him? she asked herself pointedly as her alarm started to ring. He was almost as bad as Julian Cox, although in a completely different way, of course. He had, after all, misjudged her just as badly.

Eve smiled tentatively at Kelly as Kelly opened the door to her and Brough and they stepped into the shop.

'I'll just run through a few things with you before we leave,' Kelly told her reassuringly. 'Wednesday isn't normally a very busy day so you should be okay, but if you do have any problems—'

'You've got my mobile number, haven't you, Eve?' Brough interrupted Kelly. 'Any problems and you can get in touch with Kelly on that.'

'Thank you, but I have my *own* mobile, Brough,' Kelly told him frostily.

'What I was going to say, Eve, is that I've left you the number of our landlady, Dee. She knows that you'll be working here and she may very well call in to check if everything's okay. She can be a bit daunting, but she's really very kind… She's Harry's cousin,' she added, and then stopped as Eve suddenly went bright red.

'I…I saw him—Harry—the other day when I was walking along the river,' Eve blurted out. 'I…I don't know if he mentioned it, but…'

'No. No, he didn't,' Kelly told her, before adding gently, 'But then, there's really no reason why he should…'

'No. No, of course not,' Eve told her quickly. 'I just meant… Well, I just thought…'

'We really ought to leave,' Brough informed Kelly, frowning slightly as he glanced at his watch. 'The motorway is bound to be busy.'

'I think it's wonderful what you're doing,' Eve told Kelly admiringly. 'I'd love to have that kind of talent,' she added wistfully.

'It's more of a learned skill than a natural talent,' Kelly told her wryly. 'I was just lucky enough to be in the right place to learn it at the right time, and besides, I haven't actually done anything yet.'

'No, but Brough says…' Eve stopped and glanced anxiously at her brother.

What had Brough said? Kelly wondered curiously ten minutes later as he opened the passenger door of his car for her and helped her inside.

She could always ask him, of course. Perhaps later on she would.

The Potteries where the factory was based wasn't too far up the motorway, but Kelly was still feeling extremely apprehensive about the journey. What if Brough used it as an opportunity to take her to task about her relationship with Julian? If he did, then she would just have to remind him—again—that it was none of his business, she told herself firmly as she leaned back in her seat and very deliberately closed her eyes, hoping that he would correctly interpret this as a sign that she didn't wish to talk.

Unfortunately, though, the subtleties of her body language appeared to be lost on him because almost immediately he asked her, 'Tired? I'm sorry we had to have such an early start. We should be able to stop for a short break and a cup of coffee before too long, though.'

He made it sound as though he was taking his ancient maiden aunt out for a Sunday drive, Kelly decided wrathfully, immediately sitting bolt upright in her seat and denying fiercely, 'No, I am not tired, and neither am I unable to travel a distance of less than a couple of hundred miles without the necessity of a comfort stop.'

She used the American phrase very deliberately and pointedly, underlining her comment by adding, 'I'm twenty-four, not seventy-four…'

'I, on the other hand, am thirty-four,' he told her gently, 'and *I* prefer to take life at a reasonably relaxed pace.'

Kelly gave him a surprised look. This was not the sort of comment she expected to hear from a man who had built up a business as successful as Brough's was.

'My parents died in their late thirties,' he told her tersely. 'They were killed in a plane crash. My father had been trying to get to Switzerland for an urgent business meeting and, being unable to get a scheduled flight in time, he'd hired a private plane. They got caught in a bad storm—and that was that.

'Afterwards, I made a vow to myself, a promise that I'd never forget that there was far more to life than meetings, deadlines, and making money. I was nineteen when they were killed, just an adult. Eve was six.'

Only nineteen. Kelly swallowed hard on the large knot of compassion which had lodged in her throat.

'What about you? Do you have any family?' he asked her.

'A brother who lives in South Africa with his wife and their three children. My father took early retirement and my parents normally spend the winter months in South Africa with Jamie and his family and summer at home in Scotland.'

'You're not from Rye-on-Averton? What brought you there?'

'Beth, my partner. Her godmother lives in the town and she suggested to Beth that there was an excellent business opportunity for us there. She was quite right. The shop is beginning to pick up well, and I've had several commissions, but, best of all, the way we divide things between us leaves me enough time to work on my own designs and to accept freelance stuff as well.'

'All in all, a good partnership.'

'Yes, it is,' Kelly agreed tersely. She didn't want Brough to start asking her too many questions about Beth. She had no idea whether or not he knew that Julian had been on the point of getting engaged to Beth when Eve had come into his life, and she could well imagine just what kind of assumptions Brough would make.

Unnervingly, though, he seemed to follow the direction of her thoughts because he suddenly said, 'You've said that Cox is an old friend of yours, but I get the impression from what you've just told me that your business hasn't been established very long.'

'Our accountant told us when we first started that it took three years to establish whether or not a business was going to succeed,' Kelly responded cagily.

She hated having to behave like this, she admitted. According to her family, one of her faults was that she was, at times, almost painfully honest. Prevarication of any kind was anathema to her. So why on earth had she ever allowed Dee to persuade her to adopt a role which even one minute's reflection would have told her was going to be so alien to her that it would be almost impossible to sustain? Because Dee had caught her at a weak and emotional moment, that was why.

Dee, as Kelly was fast coming to appreciate, possessed the dual gift of a very shrewd insight into people's weak points plus an ability to turn them to her own advantage. Not that she could help liking the other woman. She was, intrinsically, a very nice person. Kelly was well aware of the fact that the rent they were being charged was far less than the going amount Dee could have asked for for such a prime site, and then there had been all those little extras she had thrown in. Her concern for them had been almost sisterly and protective in many ways, and Kelly knew that they would never have made the progress they had made without Dee's help, both overt and covert. She had lost count, for instance, of the number of people who had come into the shop commenting that Dee had recommended it to them.

But that still didn't absolve her from the fact that she had deliberately used a moment of weakness to persuade Kelly into a deceit which was becoming, hourly, more stressful to maintain.

Desperate to change the subject, she asked Brough, 'Do you manage to see much of your grandmother?'

'Not as much as I'd like,' Brough admitted. 'Either

Eve or I try to get down to see her at least once a month. As it happens, we're going down the weekend after next; if you'd care to come with us you'd be more than welcome. In fact, it might actually be a good idea; that way you could see the teaset *in situ*, so to speak.'

Go with them…on a family visit…to see his grandmother?

Kelly opened her mouth and then closed it again.

'Oh, I couldn't,' she protested finally. 'There's…'

'The shop; I know,' Brough responded for her.

Had she imagined it or had that really been a note of almost cynical irony in his voice as he shot her a brief sideways glance?

It was impossible… *Anna would always stand in for you*… Hurriedly she closed her mind to the tempting little voice that was reminding her that Anna had made a point of telling her that she was more than willing to take charge of the shop during Beth's absence should Kelly want some time off.

And Brough was right in saying that it would be helpful for her to see the whole of the teaset—when she would already have had the benefit of the archivist's records.

No. No. It was completely impossible, and besides, Brough was quite obviously relieved that she hadn't accepted his invitation, because he had made no attempt to press the matter or persuade her to re-think her decision.

'The last time I drove up here I found a decent pub in a village just off the motorway at the next turn-off. Unlike you, I'm afraid I do need the odd "comfort stop",' he informed her dryly as he swung the car over from the fast lane of the motorway.

Rural Warwickshire was a part of the country with

which Kelly was relatively unfamiliar, and she couldn't quite suppress a small gasp of pleasure as they left the motorway access roundabout and Brough took an exit onto a pretty country road. Farmland stretched to either side of them, and in the distance Kelly could see the gleam of water where a river made its way between tree-lined banks.

The village, which lay concealed just beyond the brow of the hill, was reached via a meandering road which wound down to a cluster of cottages, some of which were thatched, set around a tranquil duck pond.

'Good heavens,' Kelly marvelled as Brough drove in under an archway to the rear of a pub which could quite easily have featured in a film set for a Dickens novel. 'Why on earth isn't this place swamped with tourists? It's almost too perfect...'

'It's an estate village,' Brough explained. 'Originally all the houses, like the land, were owned by the same family, but apparently when the last Earl died the new one, his grandson, decided to sell off the houses, but only to tenants who had family connections with the village.'

The pub was as quaint inside as it looked outside, and there was even a large marmalade cat sitting on an armchair in front of the empty fire.

The coffee room was cosy and prettily furnished, with windows overlooking a paved patio area filled with tubs of flowers.

When the coffee came, it arrived in a large cafetière with, Kelly noted with approval, a choice of both milk and cream—proper milk and proper cream in jugs, not fiddly little plastic containers—and there were even crisp, deliciously scented cinnamon biscuits to go with it.

As she poured herself a cup, Kelly couldn't help but notice how pleasantly Brough spoke to the waitress who had brought in the coffee for them, his manner exactly right, and she was not surprised when the girl gave him a genuinely warm smile before she left.

Kelly had only eaten out with Julian once when, by accident, she had bumped into him and Beth at a local wine bar and he had insisted on her joining them. His attitude then towards the young boy serving them had made her cringe with embarrassment and anger, and she had been unable to look Beth in the eye as she'd wondered how on earth she managed to put up with Julian's arrogant, overbearing attitude.

Kelly might be a thoroughly modern woman, but she still believed that there was a place and a need in her modern world for good manners from both sexes, and she couldn't help feeling not just a warm sense of approval for Brough's behaviour but, far more alarmingly, an additional feeling of pleasure and female pride at being with him and guessing that the waitress thought she was fortunate to be accompanied by him.

'More coffee?' Brough asked her ten minutes later when she had finished her first cup. Regretfully, Kelly shook her head. From the window she could see the river and the pathway that lay enticingly alongside it and, as though he had guessed what she was thinking, Brough commented, 'I thought we could stop here on the way back, perhaps have a bite to eat and a walk round the village, if that appeals to you.'

What could Kelly say? After his earlier display of good manners, the last thing she wanted to do was to appear gauche and ill-mannered by refusing such a pleasantly phrased invitation. It surprised her a little to discover how much she was enjoying this unexpected state of harmony which had arisen between them. When he was not cross-questioning her about Julian Cox, Brough could be very relaxing to be with.

Relaxing...? Who on earth was she kidding? Kelly asked herself a little grimly five minutes later as she checked her appearance in the ladies' cloakroom and reapplied her lipstick. If she was so relaxed then what, pray, were those goose feathers, those distinctive flutters of sensation she could feel giddying around inside her? Those sharp little darts of sensation, of reaction and warning, which kept zipping along her nervous system. If this was relaxed then she would hate to know how it felt to be really on edge in the presence of the man, she derided herself mockingly.

Admit it, she cautioned herself as she replaced the top on her lipstick, he's one very sexy man! So what? She had met sexy men before.

Met them, yes, but reacted to them in the way she was reacting to Brough, no! This was crazy, she told herself sternly. She didn't even like him. Look at how angry he had made her... Look at the things he had said to her...done to her... That kiss for instance...

Hastily Kelly looked away from the mirror and the sudden unexpected pout of her freshly lipsticked mouth.

'Okay?' Brough asked her when she rejoined him in the coffee room. The smile he gave her did uncomfortable things to her heart, causing it to somersault upwards, forwards and then backwards, leaving her breathless and slightly flushed.

'Fine,' she told him crisply, adding in a voice that was designed to show him that so far as she was concerned this was simply a business exercise and that the only thing on her mind was business, 'How long will it take us to get there?'

'Not much longer now,' Brough answered her as they made their way back to the car.

Their destination was familiar to Kelly from the time she had worked there, and as the factory gates came in sight a small, slightly rueful half-tender smile curled her mouth as she reflected on the nervous excitement of the girl she had been when she had first walked through that entrance.

'Nothing ever quite approximates the feeling of earning one's first wage packet, does it?' Brough asked her softly as they drove through the gates. 'I can remember just exactly how it felt to hold *my* first paper-round money in my hand...'

As they shared a look of mutually amused laughter his expression suddenly changed, sobering and clouding slightly.

'It concerns and grieves me that so many of our young people today will never experience the sense of self-esteem earning one's own money brings. We're in danger of creating a society of "haves" and "have nots", not merely in the material sense but in the sense of *owning* one's self-respect and self-worth which, so far as I am concerned, is almost as basic a human need as our need for air to breathe and food to eat. Like love, a strong sense of self cannot be quantified, analysed or bought, but without it our lives are empty and unfulfilled.'

His thoughts, so in tune with her own, made Kelly shiver a little as his words touched a chord within her.

It left her feeling dizzy, disorientated, as though she had somehow strayed off her normal familiar terrain, the feeling both exhilarating and frightening. The thought of what might have been had things been different trembled through her mind. That kind of bond was so rare, so precious, so…so unthinkable and impossible, she warned herself as Brough parked the car and told her mundanely, 'We're here.'

CHAPTER SEVEN

'YOU'RE very quiet. Not having second thoughts, I hope.'

They were on their way back to Rye-on-Averton, the original late-morning meeting with the archivist having turned into a full tour of the factory in addition to an inspection of its archive records, followed by an early dinner as the archivist, delighted to find a fellow enthusiast, had insisted on showing them both some examples of some of the company's rarest pieces as well as advising Kelly on just how she might best mix and colour her paints to achieve an authentic antique tone.

'Not second thoughts about wanting to do the work, just worrying about getting the paint right,' Kelly told him ruefully.

'Mmm...I must admit I hadn't realised that modern paint colours wouldn't be suitable,' Brough acknowledged. 'It's certainly a fascinating and complex business.'

'Yes,' Kelly agreed. 'I thought I knew most of what there was to know about the history of British porcelain, but listening to Frank today I realise just how wrong I was and how little I do know.'

'Mmm...I could see how thrilled he was to be able to talk with you.'

'Well, he certainly couldn't have been more helpful. But, as he says, there really isn't any substitute for seeing the rest of the teaset at first hand for ensuring that I get the colour matches right.'

'It isn't too late to change your mind about coming with us on our next visit,' Brough said.

'I…I'll have to think about it…' Kelly told him.

The evening was already turning to dusk. They had left Staffordshire just before eight o'clock. Frank Bowers had insisted on taking them out to dinner and Brough had taken her to one side after Frank had delivered his half-hesitant invitation, to say quietly to her, 'If it doesn't conflict with any other plans you may have made, I think we should accept. He's plainly enjoyed the opportunity to talk about his work—and I know we did talk about stopping off at the Lion and Swan for a meal and a walk along the river on the way back, but I should hate to disappoint Frank…'

'I agree,' Kelly had responded instantly, and they'd both returned to where Frank was putting away the company records.

'Yes, I understand you'll need to think about the weekend visit,' Brough was telling her cordially now as he swung the car out into the fast lane of the motorway. 'I should hate to interfere with any private plans you might have.'

It was the emphasis on the word 'private' that made Kelly glance warily at him. Was he trying to insinuate that he suspected her of hesitating in accepting the invitation to visit his grandmother because she was either planning to see Julian Cox or hoping to see him? It seemed that, with their return to Rye-on-Averton imminent, the cessation of hostilities between them was over.

Very well, if that was the way he wanted things, she decided hardly, suppressing the unwanted quiver of disappointment that sharpened almost to an actual pang of pain.

'I'm not sure just what you're trying to suggest,' she told him frostily, 'but the *main* reason I can't give you a yes or a no at this stage is because I need to find someone to take charge of the shop for me. *You* may be able to walk away from your business commitments for a whole weekend—I'm afraid that I can't.'

'I'm sorry,' Brough returned equally formally and coolly. 'Forgive me, but I had assumed that since this commission *was* business…'

Immediately hot colour burned a mortified flush up her throat and over her face.

'I realise that,' she retorted stiffly, and of course she did, even if very briefly earlier in the day she had momentarily forgotten.

But, in truth, hadn't there been a few brief but oh, so telling occasions during the day when the sharp line that in the past had always divided her professional life from her personal one had become dangerously blurred— when she had looked at Brough, compelled to do so by something he had said, only to find that it was not the client she was seeing but the man?

And what a man!

Kelly groaned in dismay, lashed by a delicate shiver of sexual awareness. This wasn't what she wanted, what she needed in her life right now.

Her reaction to Brough would have unnerved her even without the added complication of the situation with Julian Cox. When she added to that the already highly combustible mixture of anger and attraction she felt towards Brough, the dangerous extra ingredient of emotional awareness and longing she was confronted with became a potentially lethal cocktail which she knew could destroy her if she wasn't careful. After all, put together all those ingredients and the result was as dangerous as some magical, mystical sorcerer's potion, because the result was quite simply love. And Brough was the last person she could ever allow herself to love. He didn't like her now, so what on earth was he going to feel about her when he discovered—as discover he surely must—that she was deliberately trying to take Julian away from his sister?

She could try telling him, of course, that her motives were truly altruistic, but somehow she doubted that he would believe her, that he would even want to believe her.

'Tired?'

The unexpected concern in his voice brought a small, anguished lump to her throat. Unable to reply without betraying her emotion, she shook her head.

'It's been a long day,' Brough told her, adding ruefully, 'I must admit I had no idea of the complexity of the task I was asking you to take on when I first approached you.'

'It will be a challenge,' Kelly admitted, relieved to be back on a safer subject. 'But I am looking forward to it. My biggest worry is that your grandmother is going to be disappointed. The teaset must mean so much to her... When Frank showed us those jugs this afternoon, which had been in the same family for six generations, and he told us how much each generation had to reinsure them at, it really brought it home to me that it isn't the material value that means so much but the fact that they represent a part of a family no longer there in person, a piece of very personal history...memories...'

'Yes,' Brough agreed soberly. 'I can see from the look in Nan's eyes when she touches her teaset that it's Gramps she's thinking about.'

A little enviously Kelly wondered what it must be like

to have experienced such love, and to still be able to warm oneself by its embers.

What was Brough's grandmother like? What had his grandfather been like? Brough? Her heart gave a small, uneven thump. In thirty years from now Brough could be a grandfather himself. Her heart gave another, even more uneven thud, and then a series of short, frantic, accelerating mini-beats as she contemplated her own future. In thirty years from now how would she feel when she looked back on today? Would the sharp ache of newly discovered love for Brough she had recognised today have dulled to nothing more than a dim memory, or would she be looking back in sadness and regret for what had never been?

They were almost home now, the lights of the town shining in the valley ahead of them as Brough turned off the motorway. Kelly sat in silence beside him as he drove through the quiet streets towards the shop. Rye-on-Averton was a genteel town, its residents either middle-aged or retired in the main. Its wine bars and restaurants, though, were well patronised, as were the shows put on by the excellent local amateur dramatic and operatic societies.

'I'll come up with you,' Kelly heard Brough saying as he parked his car outside the shop.

Immediately she shook her head, but Brough was already climbing out of the car.

'It really isn't necessary,' she said as he opened her car door for her.

The flat had its own entrance, and she had already removed the keys in readiness from her bag and was holding them in her hand, but to her chagrin Brough quietly removed them from her grasp.

'I know this is a relatively crime-free and safe area,

but I'm afraid my grandmother's influence means that I would feel I had failed in my male duty if I didn't see you safely inside.'

So he was only acting out of duty. What had she imagined? she derided herself as she walked silently towards the rear entrance of the flat. That he was insisting on seeing her inside because he wanted to delay the moment when he parted from her for as long as he could? How utterly ridiculous. He probably couldn't wait to see the back of her.

'It's this way,' she told him unnecessarily, indicating the rear ground-floor door.

Stepping past her, Brough inserted the key in the lock and then opened the door for her.

'Thank you...' Kelly started to say as she stepped past him, but it seemed he still did not consider his duty to be fully done, because he shook his head and stepped into the small hallway with her, glancing towards the stairs as he did so.

'Would you like me to come up with you and look around?' he asked her politely.

Immediately, Kelly shook her head.

In the hallway on a small console table was one of the first pieces of china she had painted. She saw Brough looking at it.

'One of your pieces?' he asked her.

'Yes,' she told him. 'The inspiration for it came to me when I was on holiday in South Africa with my family.'

The piece, all greens and blues and surf-whites, always made her think of the magnificence of the Cape's beaches. Such a dramatically beautiful country with such a horrifically cruel history. She touched the curving contours of the piece of china with gentle fingers. It held many happy memories—days when she had played with her brother's children, running in and out of the surf with them, evenings when she had strolled along the beach with her parents and her brother and his wife. Very happy memories. She shuddered a little to imagine what they would think of her current involvement with Julian Cox.

'Are you cold?' Brough asked her, frowning slightly and taking a step towards her just as Kelly, too, stepped forward, away from the table.

Automatically, she put her hand out to prevent them bumping into one another as she shook her head in response to his question, but unwisely, as she did so, her gaze was drawn to his face and then his mouth.

The shape of it had been tantalising her all day—the sharp masculine cut of it, the sensual fullness of his lower lip, the dangerous and somehow illicit knowledge she had of just how it felt to have it moving on her own.

Now, just when she knew she needed to be at her coolest and most in control, her breathing had become erratic, her pulses racing, her pupils betraying the surge of feminine longing that was overpowering her.

Her brain begged her body to behave sensibly, her eyes to break contact, her breathing to slow down and become properly measured, but her senses had become flagrantly disobedient.

Very slowly Kelly lifted her gaze from Brough's mouth to his eyes. It was like gazing into deep waters, so cool that they made her body tremble as though she had touched ice, and yet so hot that her bones felt as though they were going to melt. Every sense she possessed, every centimetre of flesh covering her body, suddenly seemed to have become a thousand times more sensitive than normal, a thousand times more receptive.

She could hear Brough breathing, feel the heat of each breath he drew against her skin, sensing even the tension that coiled like fine wire through his body, feeling just what was burning through him as she gave herself up to the dark blaze of passion she could see in his eyes.

Her body swayed towards him, seeking his strength and offering in return the promise of her own pliant responsiveness, the instinctive age-old body language of woman to man, yielding and promising, whilst at the same time demanding that he show that he had the strength, the manhood, to take up the challenge she was offering and to protect her weakness.

'Brough.' She whispered his name, her eyes heavy-lidded, mysterious, luminous with passion as she turned her face up to his, an enchantress, powerful and strong. Irresistible.

And yet she still placed her hands flat against his chest, as though to deny the promise in her eyes and the desire running through her body, heavy and hot as molten gold.

She could feel his arms wrapping around her, enfolding her, as he drew her close, so close that her hand could feel the wild, fierce, heady drumming of his heartbeat, fast and furious as a cheetah during the chase. Boldly Kelly kept her eyes open. His were hot, dark, deep, glittering with male arousal.

Once again she looked at his mouth, a wild thrill of elation gripping her body. Now she was the hunter, her body tight, coiled, waiting…hungry.

Their mouths met, hers wanton, responsive, and yet at the same time soft and waiting. Brough was kissing her, sliding his hands up over her back, caressing her over and over again, his body hard and powerful against hers. Her own body felt molten and plain, reminding her of glass before it was shaped and blown, liquid running free, waiting to be formed and shaped, a wild natural element that could be coaxed but never forced.

Brough's hands were on her shoulders, gripping them hard as his tongue searched her lips for an opening. Eagerly she gave it to him, her own nails digging into the long muscles of his back.

She was experiencing a wildness within herself, a sensuality she had never encountered before, and it both exhilarated and terrified her. Beneath her clothes her breasts ached and peaked. No need for Brough to even lightly caress them to arouse her need for him, but when he did—!

Was that really her making that low, hungry, almost semi-tortured sound deep down in her throat? Was that Brough growling in fierce exultation beneath his own breath as his thumb-pad returned demandingly to caress and probe the taut peak of her nipple?

She wanted him. Wanted him…wanted him so badly. Wanted to feel his body, his skin, next to hers, his touch, his love…

Kelly made an urgent keening noise deep in her throat, her body arching against Brough's in a sexual mixture of longing and pleasure.

Somehow all the barriers there had been between them, all her doubts and fears, her refusal to believe that it was possible for her to feel like this, for her to love like this, so immediately, so intensely, so unexpectedly were banished, vaporised by the sheer force of her feelings.

Now, here in his arms, she was all feeling, yearning, loving woman, her natural female instincts overturning the conditioning of modern society and its demands. As boldly as some long-ago ancestor might have done, she was recognising and claiming for her own her man and her right to love him.

'Brough.' She whispered his name throatily, a husky purr of aroused pleasure, heavy with sensuous promise shot through with love.

'You feel so good. I want you so much...' Was that *her* saying that, or was it Brough? Was *she* the one reaching for him or was he the initiator of their increasingly passionate caresses? The shadowy confines of the hallway, normally surely the last place she would have ever thought of as romantic, now seemed as private and protected as the most secret of sanctuaries. And it was a dizzying, tantalising thought to know that not so very far beyond its closed door lay her bedroom—her bed.

Her whole body shuddered as it wantonly followed where her thoughts were leading, where she already ached for Brough to lead her. A feeling of the most incandescent joy filled her; a sense of throwing off the past and turning to welcome the future and their love made her feel as though suddenly something unacknowledged deep within her had sprung to life, as though the person she had been before the wonderful, miraculous discovery that she loved Brough had been someone who was only half alive, someone who had been deprived of the true pleasures and meaning of life.

'I don't want you to go...'

As she murmured the words against Brough's mouth she could feel him start to tense; his mouth left her throat, which he had been kissing and nibbling, sending a cascade of tiny erotic shivers all the way from the top of her head to her toes.

'I don't want to either,' he whispered back as his thumb caressed her throat and then her jaw, slowly moving towards her mouth. 'But I must. I'm expecting a call from Hong Kong—I had some business dealings there, which I've sold out of, but there are still some legal ends I need to tie up. And tomorrow I have to go to London to see my accountants. But when I come back…'

As he turned away he paused and then turned back, taking hold of her hand and urging her gently towards him.

'Thank you…' he told her softly.

'For what?' she managed to ask him in a shaky voice.

'For today…and this…and you…' he told her throatily as he bent to place a soft kiss on her half-parted lips.

For *her*… For a moment Kelly felt close to tears. There was so much more about her that he still didn't know. So much that she still had to tell him—especially… But now, when he was on the point of leaving, wasn't the time to start explaining about Julian and Beth.

'I know you're only being like this because you're worried about how much I'm going to charge you for the teaset,' she told him teasingly and a little chokily.

'Aha…so you've seen through my dastardly plot, then,' Brough responded in the same vein.

Suddenly anxious, she clung to him and whispered, 'Oh, Brough, it's all so new, so unexpected. I don't…'

'It's perfect…*you're* perfect,' Brough assured her as he tightened his arms around her and cradled her head against his shoulder. '*We* are going to be perfect…together… Right now, there's nothing I want more than to stay here with you.'

He looked betrayingly towards the inner doorway to the flat and, guessing what he was thinking, Kelly quickly reassured him. 'I know and I understand. You've got your responsibilities, and anyway, perhaps… Everything's happened so quickly, so…'

'I'll call you the moment I get back from London,' Brough promised her huskily.

'There's so much I haven't told you,' Kelly protested as he started to release her.

'Such as?' Brough grinned. 'I've already discovered for myself all that I need to know, and what I have discovered, what I do know...I love...'

'Oh, Brough...'

It was impossible not to throw herself back into his arms and share another passionate kiss with him, and then he was gone, leaving her to touch her fingertips to a mouth that still tingled from the passion of his kiss and to acknowledge with a small, cold shiver that he was wrong, that there were things that he still had to learn.

Would it change what he thought, what he felt, when he learned of her deceit, or would he understand and accept that her deliberate pursuit of Julian had been prompted by loyalty to Beth?

CHAPTER EIGHT

'So YOU do understand, Dee, don't you?' Kelly asked the older woman anxiously as they sat opposite one another in Kelly's flat.

Kelly had telephoned Dee as soon as Brough had left, despite the fact that it was late evening. The disquiet she had experienced over the role she was playing *vis-à-vis* Julian had coalesced following Brough's departure into a sharp and intense need to free herself from the restrictions that her commitment to Dee's plans were placing on her. There was no way she wanted to deceive Brough, and there was certainly no way she could even pretend now to be anything other than totally revolted by Julian Cox.

'I think so,' Dee confirmed dryly. 'You're telling me that you've fallen in love with Brough Frobisher and that because of that you don't want to carry out your part of our scheme.'

'It isn't that I don't *want* to,' Kelly corrected her quietly, 'it's that I *can't*; and even before I realised how I felt about Brough... I'm not trying to be dramatic, Dee, but there's something about Julian I just don't trust.'

'Join the club,' Dee told her sardonically. 'I don't want to cast a shadow over love's sweet dream, Kelly, and you're certainly old enough and I believe mature enough to be the best judge of your own feelings, but Brough is Eve's brother, and he *does* have a vested interest in monitoring your relationship with Julian therefore.'

Kelly looked at her for several seconds before asking her sternly, 'What are you trying to say? That Brough is deliberately and callously pretending to…to care about me because he wants to leave his sister with a clear field to Julian Cox?'

'No. What I'm *trying* to say is that you would be well advised and wise to be aware that things are not perhaps as straightforward as they could be, that people do have hidden motives and personal agendas for what they do. After all, on the face of it, so far as Brough is concerned, he has a potential rival for your love in Julian, hasn't he?'

'I wanted to explain to him but I just didn't have the chance, and then I decided that I owed it to you to let you know what I intended to do first,' Kelly told her quickly.

She had found it extremely unsettling and disturbing listening to what Dee had to say. Dee was wrong, of course; Brough would never do anything like that… Would he?

'I know you must feel that I'm letting you down,' Kelly told Dee quietly.

'I'm disappointed, yes,' Dee acknowledged, 'but I *do* understand. I have been in love myself, you know, and I do—' She broke off, and to Kelly's surprise she saw that the older girl's face was slightly flushed.

Why?

Dee was only thirty, and what could be more natural, after all, than that she should have experienced falling in love?

'I can't pretend that I don't wish you'd change your mind,' Dee continued honestly, 'but at least Julian seems to be biting on the bait so far as Anna is concerned. Anna was able to ''accidentally' bump into him at yesterday's mayoral function, and vaguely mentioned that she had recently received rather a large sum of money from an insurance policy which had matured and that she was looking for somewhere to invest it with a view to making the maximum amount of profit.'

'You do realise, don't you,' Kelly said a little uncomfortably, 'that I'm going to have to say *something* to Brough about our…about what we planned?'

Dee's eyebrows rose.

'Dear me, it *is* love, isn't it?' she acknowledged dryly. 'I appreciate what you're saying, Kelly,' she responded firmly, 'but I would at least ask you to keep my part in our plans to a discreet minimum. I'm sure your Brough isn't one to tittle-tattle or gossip, but I *do* have a certain position within our local community and I wouldn't want our plans bruited about.

'I personally believe that Julian Cox deserves all that we planned for him and more, that what we intended to do doesn't come to even one tenth of the punishment he deserves, but I have to be honest and admit that there *are* people who might take a very different view, and I certainly don't want to be judged as some sort of melodramatic woman, bent on exacting revenge for some imagined slight…'

'Oh, I'm sure Brough would never think that,' Kelly assured her, so quick to defend her beloved.

'Maybe,' Dee acknowledged, 'but others might.'

'Well, if you prefer it, I could simply say that we'd all agreed that Julian needed to be taught a lesson,' Kelly offered.

'I thought that was what we *had* all agreed,' Dee commented wryly as she stood up.

'One thing that does still worry me,' Kelly told her

as she followed her to the flat door, 'and that's Eve, Brough's sister. She's desperately in love with Julian...'

'And he, by all accounts, is still desperate to secure her—if he can't get you,' Dee concluded. 'I certainly don't envy you *that* relationship, Kelly...Julian Cox as your brother-in-law by marriage.'

'Oh, no, don't say that,' Kelly pleaded with her. 'He'd make Eve so dreadfully unhappy. Maybe I should try to talk to her, warn her...tell her what he did to Beth.'

'Do you think she would listen?' Dee asked her doubtfully. 'Julian's told so many lies, it might be hard to convince her.'

'I've only met her a couple of times,' Kelly said, 'but she strikes me as someone who would think deeply about the situation if we put it to her.'

'Mmm... You and Harry both. He's been singing her praises to me ever since the night of the ball. When are you seeing Brough again, by the way?'

'I don't know. He's going to London on business in the morning, but he said he'd get in touch just as soon as he could.'

'Goodnight, then,' Dee told her as she opened the flat door and stepped out into the fresh air.

Dee had parked her car quite close to the shop, but instead of going directly to it she chose, instead, to walk in the opposite direction through the town and down towards the river.

The walk along the river path had been one of her favourites as a girl. It had been her route home from school and, later on when she had gone to university, it had been one of the first places she had headed for on her return home.

Her family had lived in the area for many generations;

her mother had died shortly after Dee's birth and her father, older than her mother by some eighteen years, had died just before Dee was about to take her degree.

She had returned home to sort out his affairs and to discover that she was an extremely wealthy young woman.

One of the first things she had done with her money had been to make a large, interest-free loan to her uncle in order to enable him to modernise the family farm and buy more land.

Her own father, his brother, had sold his share of the family farmland as a young man, preferring to deal and speculate in the commodities market rather than follow the custom of his forebears, and it had seemed to Dee to be a good memorial to him that she should help her uncle to buy back the land he had sold away from the family. The two brothers had never quarrelled over his decision, and had always got on amicably for two such very, very different people, but Dee, who had inherited her father's intelligence, knew that it was becoming increasingly difficult for small farmers to make a decent living and she had seen that there could come a time when her uncle, for financial reasons, would either have to sell up or rent out his lands.

With the rest of the money she had made several donations to local charities, and then amused herself by finding out if she had inherited her father's gift for making the right investment.

It had turned out that she had.

But, at twenty-one, a girl wanted far more from life than a healthy bank balance, and Dee had had all the normal urges and needs of her sex and age—a man to love and love her, the prospect of a relationship that would last a lifetime and one which included commitment, children...love...

And, for all too brief a space of time, while she had been at university, she had thought she had that relationship...that love...*had* thought...but had thought wrongly. Had made the worst, the most disastrous decision of her life, had prejudiced everything she had, everything she was, because of someone who had proved to be so false, so cruelly betraying that even now she still bore the scars.

She stopped walking, shoving her hands deep into the pockets of her lightweight jacket, and stared angrily up towards the stars.

She had waited a long time for this opportunity to turn the tables on Julian Cox, to get him in a position where he was vulnerable and unable to protect himself...as she had once been. Oh, yes, she had been vulnerable...

Fiercely she bit down hard on her bottom lip. She wasn't being vindictive, she was simply exercising her right to have justice, avenging the wrong which had been done to her, and neither were her motives totally selfish. She *had* been concerned for Beth's pain and heartbreak and, despite what Kelly seemed to think, she was aware of the difficult position she had potentially put her in, and of the heartache that Eve could suffer if no one warned her what Julian was.

She had, of course, assumed that Eve would immediately refuse to have anything further to do with Julian once his involvement with Kelly became public knowledge; Brough would have surely insisted on that for his sister's own sake and, from what she knew of him, Brough was certainly a strong enough character to be able to achieve that end.

It was a pity that Kelly had changed her mind, but the

game wasn't over yet, not by a long chalk. One way or another, Dee was determined that Julian Cox was going to make full recompense for the debt he owed her. *Full* recompense…with interest, the interest at the punitively high rate caused by the sheer extent and weight of the emotional anguish and despair she had suffered.

There was no despair like that of suffering a broken heart, destroyed dreams, the complete desolation of a once promising future.

Determinedly, Dee started to head back towards the town centre. It was time for her to go home. Yes, Kelly's decision was going to cause her a problem, but no problem was insurmountable unless you allowed it to be and she, Dee, was certainly not going to do that.

Where was Brough now? Kelly wondered dreamily as she said goodbye to the customer she had just served. In another five minutes she was going to close the shop for the day and then she was going to go upstairs and indulge in the delicious pleasure of curling up in a chair whilst she relived every second of yesterday, and most especially what had happened after Brough had insisted on seeing her safely inside the flat.

Even now she felt as though it couldn't be real, as though she had to keep mentally pinching herself to make sure she wasn't imagining everything.

She *had* felt guilty telling Dee that she couldn't go on with their plans, but wisely Kelly knew that even without the discovery of her love for Brough she would have found it extremely difficult to continue to practise the deceit her role had called for.

Where was Brough? Still in London? On his way back? When would she hear from him…see him… hold him?

She caught her breath as she heard the shop doorbell ring behind her, and out of the corner of her eye she caught the male outline of the person walking in.

'Brough!'

She turned round eagerly, his name on her lips, only to be swept by a surge of disappointment as she recognised that her visitor wasn't Brough but Julian.

'What happened to you last night?' Julian demanded without preamble. 'We had a date...at the wine bar...remember?'

Guiltily Kelly frowned. She had completely forgotten about that, but even if she hadn't... The last person she really wanted to see was Julian Cox, but since he was here she could at least make it abundantly clear to him just where she stood, and, turning away from him so that he couldn't see her face, she managed a dismissive shrug.

'I changed my mind,' she told him carelessly. 'In fact...'

Summoning all her courage, she turned round and announced crisply, 'In fact, Julian, I think it would be best if you didn't try to get in touch with me any more.'

'What are you trying to say?' Julian demanded furiously, his mouth tightening as he stepped in front of her, blocking her exit. She couldn't do this to him. He had got it all planned—Kelly, with her substantial fortune, unfettered by any access restrictions, was a much better proposition than Eve with her trust fund and her brother, and besides, he wanted Kelly. She excited him in a way that the Beths and Eves of this world could never do.

'I'm trying to say that I think we've both made a mistake,' Kelly informed him as diplomatically as she could. 'You are dating someone else...'

'So?' Julian demanded. '*You* didn't seem to consider

that much of a problem the other night at the ball, nor when I rang you up...'

'Maybe not,' Kelly allowed. 'But since then I've had time to think things through... Eve loves you, Julian,' she told him directly.

To her disbelief, instead of looking embarrassed, he smiled triumphantly.

'You're jealous, aren't you?' he challenged her. 'Well, you needn't be. Eve's a child, Kelly, but you're a woman... The things you and I could do...' he promised her thickly. 'You know what I mean. You want them too. I've seen it in your eyes... Eve is a mistake. It's you I want, Kelly.'

Thoroughly revolted, Kelly tried to step back from him, but the hard edge of the counter was behind her, jarring her back. She looked anxiously towards the door, wishing a customer would walk in and put an end to their unwanted privacy. Unwanted on her part, that was. Julian, far from accepting what she had told him, seemed to be trying to be deliberately obtuse, Kelly recognised. Was he really so vain that he didn't realise how much she loathed him? If so, she would simply have to take a stronger line with him.

'Julian, I meant what I said,' she told him firmly. 'I don't want to see you. If I gave you the wrong idea—'

'*If?*' he broke in, his face changing as he understood the forcefulness of her determination. No way could he afford to let her go, he acknowledged inwardly. When he had first met Eve he had not realised just how much control her brother had over her financial affairs. There was no love lost between him and Brough at all.

'You were giving me the green light, Kelly, all the way to your bedroom door. I want you, Kelly, and I intend to have you.'

'No!' Kelly protested, shocked.

'Oh, come on,' he overrode her. 'You want me too; I can see it in your eyes…your mouth…' As he spoke he reached out and pressed his thumb hard against her bottom lip. 'There's no way I'm going to let you go.'

Taken off guard, Kelly immediately tried to push him away, making a sharp sound of distress.

He actually made her feel physically sick, and not just sick but afraid as well, she recognised as she saw the ugly look in his eyes.

'I want you to leave, Julian,' she told him shakily. 'Now…'

'Oh, you do, do you?' he responded aggressively. 'And what if I choose not to? What if *I* choose to make *you* come good on all those sexy promises you've been giving me, Kelly? What are you going to do about it? How are you going to stop me?'

'What you're talking about is sexual harassment,' Kelly told him bravely. 'If you don't stop threatening me and leave straight away, Julian, I shall report you to the police.'

To her dismay, instead of responding as she'd hoped, he threw back his head and laughed.

'Do you think they'd believe you…after the way you've been coming on to me? Get real, Kelly. You're just being hysterical.'

Hysterical—wasn't that what he had accused Beth of being?

Outrage and panic paralysed Kelly, rooting her feet to the floor as she stood trapped in the maniacal beam of his almost colourless, cold eyes.

Julian was a desperate man, she recognised numbly. He was also *enjoying* her fear, feeding off it, not just emotionally, she sensed with increasing, horrified disgust and fear, but physically as well. Oh, please God, let someone come into the shop and save her, she prayed mentally as she fought not to succumb to the awful, fearful heaviness filling her body. To say that she was afraid in no way came even close to describing what she felt. Her whole body had gone icy cold. She knew, she just *knew*, that Julian meant every word he said, that nothing, nothing she could do or say would persuade him to leave. Now, when it was almost too late, she recognised how much she had underestimated how dangerous he really was.

Brough had been delayed in London longer than he had planned. There had been a couple of time-consuming delays in the finalisation of the transaction with Hong Kong. He had been tempted to ring Kelly just as he left the city, but he had wanted to clear his mind of everything to do with his work before he spoke to her again. And besides, when he told her he loved her he wanted to see the look in her eyes, to hear that wonderful female adorable catch in her breath as she looked at him, to know that she felt the same way that he did.

Impossible now to think that he had imagined that first time he had held her in his arms that he was immune to the risk of falling in love—and besides, *what* risk? Loving her was *heaven…paradise…*the fulfilment of his every previously unacknowledged dream.

He would go home, shower and then drive round and see her…surprise her…

So why, having made that decision, did he suddenly, when he was within a hundred yards of his own driveway, suddenly succumb to an almost overpowering sense of urgency, so strong a need, so immediate and intense, that he drove through a set of traffic lights on amber and broke the speed limit just to get to her. He drew up several yards away from the flat and got out, forgetting to lock his car as he strode quickly towards the shop.

As he approached the door he could see two people inside. Kelly was standing with her back half turned towards him so that he could only partially see her face, her head submissively bent towards the man who was wrapping his arms around her. To anyone else their pose might have seemed to be that of lovers, but Brough knew immediately and incontrovertibly that it wasn't love that was keeping Kelly immobile in Julian Cox's embrace, but fear. Just *how* he knew it he didn't stop to question as he pushed open the door and rushed to Kelly's side, forcibly thrusting Julian away from her. As he did so he could see not just the relief and shock in her eyes, but also an anguished pain that cut right to his heart. His love, his darling, felt shamed by the fact that she was being attacked by...

He could quite happily have slowly roasted Julian Cox over a very, very hot fire, just for that act of violation alone—he, a man of peace and logic. Brough could see the fury and the fear in the other man's eyes, and the urge to punish him, hurt and frighten him, as well as release his own fury against him, was so strong that for a second Brough was almost tempted to give in to it.

But over Julian's shoulder he could see where Kelly was standing, white-faced, her eyes blank with shock, and instead he released Julian and told him in disgust, 'Get out of here before I give in to the temptation to forget that non-violence is the making of a truly intelligent man.'

'You've got it all wrong...' Julian started to whine as he backed towards the door. 'She's the one who's to blame, not me. She's the one who's been leading me on, coming on to me,' he started to protest, but Brough had heard enough. Grabbing hold of his collar, he virtually marched him to the door and opened it, pushing him through it.

'If I find out you've so much as even tried to speak to her again, I promise you you're going to regret it,' he told Julian in a steely voice.

As Brough locked the door he turned towards Kelly. She was still standing motionless, her face grey-white, her eyes huge and unfocused. *She* was his prime concern now. He could talk to her later, find out later just what had been going on and why Cox had been terrorising her.

At the back of his mind as he walked towards Kelly lay the knowledge that he was now going to have to take very firm action over Julian's relationship with his sister, but right now Kelly was his only priority.

'Kelly... It's all right, my darling, he's gone, you're safe...'

As she heard Brough's familiar, warm voice, Kelly turned her head and looked towards him, towards him but not at him. How could she? How could she *ever* come to terms with the pain, the humiliation, the defilement of what she had just experienced? Julian's verbal attack on her, his threatened assault on her, had left her feeling totally physically shocked and degraded. The thought passed through her mind that if this was how *she* felt how on earth did rape victims feel? How did *they* cope? Julian's abuse of her had come nowhere close to anything like that...

'Come on...I'm taking you upstairs...' she heard Brough telling her. Desperately she struggled to get back to normality, her always keen sense of responsibility reminding her of her duties.

'I can't—the shop,' she began to protest, but Brough overruled her.

'The shop is closed,' he told her firmly, adding more gently, 'You're in shock, my love; there's no way you can work. You need…' He paused and started to frown. 'Who is your GP? I think perhaps that…'

Immediately Kelly shook her head.

'No, no, I'm fine…' Her bottom lip started to tremble. 'Honestly, Brough, I will be fine,' she told him in a thready voice. 'I don't need… I don't want… It was my own fault,' she told him huskily, dropping her head so that he couldn't look into her eyes and see the truth she felt must be clear there. 'I shouldn't have—'

'You shouldn't have what?' Brough interrupted her immediately and fiercely. 'You shouldn't have let him in? No way was it your fault, Kelly. I *saw* what was going on… There was *no way* you were inviting or enjoying what was going to happen.'

The sureness in his voice, the conviction, the trust and the love were too much for Kelly's fragile composure. Hot tears filled her eyes and started to roll down her face as she shook her head.

'Oh, no, please, my love, don't cry,' Brough begged her with a small groan. 'I shouldn't have let him walk away from this… The police…'

'No…no, please. I don't want anything like that,' Kelly protested sharply. 'I just want to forget about it, Brough… I just want…'

She started to tremble violently, reaction setting in as the realisation of what had happened swamped her.

'Come on, I'm taking you up to your flat,' Brough

told her masterfully, holding her gently by the arm and leading her towards the door.

Five minutes later she was standing in her own small kitchen drinking the fortifying mug of coffee Brough had just made her, liberally laced with brandy. She could feel the strong spirit going straight to her head, relaxing her both physically and emotionally, releasing her from the rigid self control she had been exercising ever since Julian Cox had walked into the shop.

'Brough, Julian wanted...' she began huskily, suddenly desperately anxious to tell him everything, to explain to him what she had been doing and why, but before she could finish what she had been about to say she suddenly became very dizzy.

Immediately Brough reached for her, rescuing the half-empty mug she had been about to drop, gathering her in his arms as he told her gruffly, 'I know *exactly* what Cox wanted... He's gone, Kelly. You're safe— forget about him...'

'No, you don't understand,' Kelly protested, but it was impossible to keep on trying to form rational thoughts and make difficult and painful explanations when Brough was holding her so tightly, one hand stroking her hair whilst the other tilted up her chin so that he could look down into her eyes.

'I should *never* have gone home and left you last night,' he whispered rawly to her. 'I certainly didn't want to...'

'*I* didn't want you to either,' Kelly admitted bravely, adding tremulously, 'Oh, Brough, I wanted you to stay so much, but...I still can't quite believe all this is happening...that you and I... It frightens me a little,' she admitted, her tongue as well as her self-control loosened by the potent mixture of shock and alcohol. 'I've never been in love before, never wanted... Loving someone means risking that they might hurt you and—'

'I could *never* hurt you, Kelly,' Brough interrupted her to tell her passionately. 'And I know that you would never hurt me.'

'How *can* you know that?' Kelly protested nervously. 'Brough, there's so much about me that you don't know...'

'Mmm...so much about you that I still have to discover...' Brough agreed softly as his lips started to caress her willing mouth.

'Brough...' Kelly whispered, but it was only a token protest. There was nothing she wanted more than to be held like this by him, kissed like this by him, unless it was to lie naked in bed with him, his body her only covering, his hands caressing her, leaving hers free to explore him...

'Mmm...well, if you're sure that's what you want, I'm certainly not going to argue with you,' she heard Brough saying hoarsely as he gently stepped back from her and turned her to face the kitchen door, and it was only then that Kelly realised that what she had thought were her most private and unspoken thoughts she had in fact spoken out loud to him.

'Oh, Brough...'

Her face pink, she looked helplessly at him, but far from being shocked by the desires and wishes she had expressed he was looking at her as though...as though... Kelly felt her heartbeat start to pick up. Suddenly she was finding it extraordinarily difficult to breathe properly; suddenly her mind was full of the most extraordinarily detailed and sensual images of them both together; suddenly she couldn't wait to make those private wanton thoughts a reality.

It took them almost ten minutes to reach the bedroom, primarily because Brough insisted on stopping virtually every foot of the way to hold her and kiss her and tell her that she was the most wonderful, the most wanted thing that had ever happened to him.

'I never imagined you could be like this,' Kelly breathed in ecstatic pleasure as the look in his eyes confirmed that he meant every romantic word he was saying to her. 'When we first met, you seemed so disapproving…so…'

'So desperately afraid of revealing to you just how totally and completely I'd fallen for you,' Brough admitted softly as he cupped her face and very slowly started to kiss her.

Dizzily Kelly clung to him. They were in her bedroom now, and Brough was very carefully, but *very* thoroughly and determinedly, starting to remove her clothing whilst continuing to kiss her with a passion which caused her heartbeat to slow to a sensuously heavy thud and her body to melt into eager compliance and longing.

This was not how it was meant to be for a modern nineties woman. *She* was supposed to take her own initiative, remove her *own* clothes and expect her lover to remove his with equally mature independence, and when a modern woman did make love it was an open-eyed, clear-minded 'I know what I'm doing and why' thing. Wasn't it?

So *why* was she, who considered herself to be such a thoroughly modern woman, simply standing there, not merely allowing Brough to dictate the pace of their lovemaking but positively *yearning* for him to do so? *Why* was she experiencing this unfamiliar, heady sense of pleasure and excitement, of anticipation and, yes, just a tiny thread of nervousness as well, at the thought of what lay ahead? Why, much as she wanted him, ached for him, *loved* him, did she actually want *him* to be the one, initially at least, to show her how much he loved and wanted her?

Because she loved him enough to do so! Because she trusted him enough! Because there was, after all, something inalienably sweet and precious about admitting, *allowing* herself to be so vulnerably female in his presence, in being able, for the first time since childhood, to acknowledge a need for another person, for their love…their touch…

'Brough…'

She shivered in delicious pleasure as he slid her top away from her body and then gently unclipped her bra, freeing her breasts to his gaze and the softness of the air against them. As she felt and saw her nipples peak into hard, excited, aroused nubs of flesh, Kelly knew immediately what was responsible for their arousal—or rather who. It wasn't cold in her bedroom and, anyway, she undressed in here every night without her body reacting like this.

'Beautiful…beautiful…' Brough murmured thickly as he reached out and gently traced the curve of one breast, brushing its softness with his finger, the lightest of light touches, and yet it was enough to send a sensuous shudder of sensation curling through her entire body.

'Beautiful,' Brough repeated as he bent his head and, cupping her breast very carefully, kissed one erect nipple and then the other, and then repeated the whole process again and then again, and each time his mouth returned to graze and suckle on one swollen point the other ached jealously for the loss of the delicious pressure of his mouth against it.

'Brough…'

Heavy-eyed, Kelly bent her head towards him, leaning its weight on his downbent shoulder. Beneath her cheek she could feel the fabric of his shirt. Quickly she started to pull it free of his waistband, making a little frustrated sound of protest deep in her throat, a small feline growl of longing as she realised that unless and until she unfastened the buttons of his shirt and physically removed it from his body she was going to be denied the sensation of his skin against her own which she craved so much. But if she did that he might have to stop kissing and caressing her breasts in that delicious way.

But somehow Brough seemed to have divined her thoughts, because he gently eased her slightly away from him, kissing her deeply on the mouth as he lifted her hands to the front of his shirt and then, whilst he was still kissing her, placed his own hands over her breasts, gently teasing her erect nipples with his thumbs and fingertips. Already sensitised by the erotic attention of his mouth, they reacted to this extra stimulation by causing such a curling, coiling, tightening feeling to gather deep inside her body that Kelly cried out in soft protest against the intensity of what she was feeling.

Her fingers stilled over the task of unfastening his shirt and then, as the sensation within her body refused to be controlled, her actions quickened, becoming urgent and demanding, her lips pressing tiny hungry kisses against Brough's jaw, his throat, and then lower, following the reckless speed of her fingers as she tugged and wrenched at the recalcitrant buttons, the progress of both her hands and her mouth only halted when she suddenly realised that she had reached the barrier of his belt.

Now it was Brough who was losing control, groaning rawly as he took her hands and guided them over his body. The feel of him even through the fabric of his clothes, hard, hot and aroused, filled her own insides with a heaviness, a dull, unfamiliar ache, and an instinctive knowledge that there was only one way, one way it was going to be eased...satisfied...

Kelly needed no encouragement nor coaxing to remove the rest of his clothes. Now she *was* an all nineties woman, wanting her man and not ashamed for him to know it, proud of her own body, her own sexuality as he stripped the rest of her clothes from it with a fierce eagerness that matched and fed her own longing.

When they were both completely naked she looked at him and then told him breathlessly—and meant it, 'Brough, you are *so* beautiful. So perfect...' Hot-faced with female appreciation, she ran a delicate but oh, so possessive fingertip down the length of him, teasingly avoiding the thick dark shaft of aroused manhood that was almost awesomely powerful to her as a woman—in some ways an almost primitive visual reminder of the human race's sexuality and its genetically encoded gift and goal of ensuring its own continuity—and yet still somehow a reminder of how very vulnerable a man could be, how very much in need of a woman's love and even of her protection of his maleness, of her appreciation of it and of him.

Very, very gently and carefully, caringly, Kelly reached out and ran her fingertip the entire length of the engorged shaft, lovingly circling its tip, smiling a mysterious, sultry, female smile of power and love as she caught Brough's audibly indrawn breath and saw the fierce leap of passion darkening his eyes before he closed them on a helpless moan of aching male pleasure.

'Oh, God, that feels so good,' he told her throatily, and then, opening his eyes, he admitted, 'Too good, Kelly; if you do it again I don't know...'

'You don't know what?' Kelly teased, obliging him with an opportunity to find out as she delicately ran her fingertip back up the way it had just come.

'I don't know whether to kiss you…or…'

Far too quickly for Kelly to stop him, he grabbed hold of her, rolling her down onto the bed and very gently keeping her there as he carefully parted her thighs, kissing the inner flesh of each one before looking up at her uncertain face and smiling tenderly at her.

'No,' Kelly protested, guessing what he was going to do and knowing instinctively that once she felt his lips, his mouth against that most vulnerable and sensuously responsive part of her body there was no way she was going to be able to hold back the response that had been building up inside her ever since their first kiss.

But of course she knew that Brough wasn't going to listen to her denial, and she knew as well that there was no way she really wanted him to do so.

The gentle brush of his lips against the soft mound of her sex was the most blissful, the most sensual, the most erotic and achingly beautiful sensation she had ever experienced, she told herself dizzily. And then, for good measure, she told Brough as well, interspersing the words with soft, husky, imploring pleas for him to stop before…because… Her voice finally trailed away into a soft sob of delirious pleasure as the dragging ache inside her changed shape and texture and form and became a living, pulsing, fiery sensation that exploded sharply inside her in a cataclysmic surge of pleasure which to her surprise left her not drained and empty but somehow feeling as though she was just on the edge of some previously unguessed and undreamed-of new universe of delight, heralded by the tiny but unmistakable little excited pulse that still throbbed inside her body.

Very gently, but very determinedly, she urged Brough towards her.

'I want you,' she told him shakily. 'I want you now, Brough…'

'Now,' he repeated, but he was already responding to her, answering her, his body starting to move within hers slowly and then with gathering pace, gathering force, so that with each thrust he lifted her and carried her a little further, a little closer towards the goal her body now so desperately craved.

'Yes, now,' she whispered back. 'Now, Brough… now…now… Oh, Brough… Brough… Brough…'

She could feel the world exploding around her, the whole universe filling with light and love and Brough.

Brough… Brough whom she loved so much, whom she would always love so much…who loved her…

Satisfied, satiated, Kelly snuggled down into his arms. Sleepily she remembered that there was something she had to tell him, something she had to say…something…

Her eyes were already closed, her breathing slowing…

Tenderly Brough curled her into the warmth of his own relaxed body.

There had been a moment, a heartbeat, just then, when, just before the end, he had felt his eyes start to burn with emotional tears. Strange how, until he had met her, he had never even known how much he had wanted to find her, how desperately he must secretly have been searching for her… How good and right she would feel and how complete she would make his life.

He must remember to tell Eve that when he was trying to explain to her why Julian Cox wasn't the man for her. Kelly!

God, but he loved her…had loved her, he now recognised, the moment he saw her, even though she had been behaving in a way which he now knew was way, way out of character. He started to frown. There were still things they needed to discuss. She had originally claimed Cox as an old friend, but the way he had been behaving towards her earlier had been anything but friendly.

His frown deepened as he heard a familiar sound from the landing where he had left his jacket. Gently easing his body away from Kelly's, so as not to disturb her, he padded towards it, flicking the receiving switch on his mobile phone. An unfamiliar voice on the other end of the line announced that he was Brough's grandmother's GP.

'She's had a fall—a neighbour found her. We've admitted her to hospital, but unfortunately she's developed pneumonia. It can happen with elderly patients…'

'I'm on my way,' Brough told him grimly.

Back in the bedroom, he quickly dressed. Kelly stirred in her sleep and opened her eyes, frowning as she saw what he was doing.

Still half asleep, she questioned anxiously, 'Brough…?'

'It's all right,' he told her. 'Go back to sleep. I've got to go… I'll explain later…'

Her eyes were already closing again. She was exhausted, he recognised, the shock of Cox's attack on her no doubt now taking its toll along with the brandy he had given her and the intensity and passion of their lovemaking.

His mind raced ahead. He would have to tell Eve about their grandmother. But he didn't want the additional delay of driving home. He would call her on his mobile. Dear God, but he hoped Nan was going to be all right. She was a fighter, he knew that, but a serious fall at her age, followed by the complication of pneumonia... No wonder the doctor had sounded so grave.

Quietly Brough let himself out of Kelly's flat and headed for his car.

CHAPTER NINE

'AND you're sure that Nan's going to be all right?'

'Yes, Eve, the doctors say she's over the worst now, and although they want to keep her in hospital for observation they're confident that she's on the mend,' Brough assured his sister gently as he heard the concern in her voice.

He had arrived at the hospital just as his grandmother's pneumonia entered its most critical stage and had sat with her, willing her to draw strength from him and pull through, holding her hand tightly in his, even though the doctor had told him kindly that she was probably not aware of his presence. At one point she had turned her head, opening her eyes as she looked at him, and Brough had felt his eyes smart with tears as she'd called him by his grandfather's, her late husband's, name.

It was now ten o'clock at night, three hours and ten minutes since he had left Kelly. He was longing to speak with her, and longing even more to be with her, but first he had an important brotherly duty to perform.

'Eve, I appreciate that this might not be a good time to tell you this. You know that I've never been exactly happy about your relationship with Julian Cox, but I've no—'

'Brough, before you go any further, there's something I have to tell you,' Eve interrupted him nervously.

Brough felt his heart sink. He knew how loyal she was, and how trusting, how stubborn as well, but surely if he told her that he had actually found Julian attacking Kelly…

'Eve—' he began.

But she overruled him, begging shakily, 'Brough, please let me speak. I'm so nervous about telling you this, but I'm legally an adult now, and we've both talked the whole thing through, and even if you, as my trustee, withhold the allowance from my trust fund from me it wouldn't stop us. We love each other, Brough, and we want to be together. We *have* to be together. Oh, Brough, I love him so much,' she told him, the emotion in her voice so strong that Brough almost felt the air around him humming with it. 'If you'd ever been in love yourself, you'd understand… I don't want you to hate me for what I'm doing, but even if you do…'

Brough closed his eyes and took a deep breath. He hated having to do what he was going to have to do…hated having to destroy her dreams…her love, but what option did he have when he knew what Cox really was?

'Eve,' he said gently. 'I'm sorry, I understand everything you're saying, and you're wrong—I do understand what it means to be in love, to love someone; but you can't marry Julian Cox.'

The silence that followed his announcement was so complete and so intense that for a moment Brough thought she had actually hung up, and then he heard her saying shakily, 'Brough, I'm sorry; I haven't…I didn't… It isn't Julian I'm in love with…'

Now it was Brough's turn to be silent.

Not Cox. Then who? What…?

'It's Harry,' Eve blurted out.

'Harry!' Brough repeated in bemusement. 'Harry—'

'Harry Lawson,' Eve explained, adding earnestly, 'You remember he was at the ball we went to…'

'You mean the Harry who was escorting Kelly?' Brough questioned her sharply.

'Yes. But there's nothing between *them*. He was simply escorting her because his cousin had asked him to,' Eve told him defensively, before adding eagerly, 'Oh, Brough, I love him so much and so, I know, will you.'

'Yes… Yes…I'm sure I shall,' Brough agreed obediently, mentally reviewing what little he knew of Harry. A pleasant, solid-looking young man, phlegmatic in the extreme, Brough would have guessed, reliable, solid, trustworthy, an excellent foil for his sister's far more vulnerable and fragile personality.

A sense of relief began to fill him as he digested what he had just learned.

'Tell me again that Nan is going to be all right,' Eve implored, adding, 'I want to come down and see her, Brough, and I want to bring Harry with me.'

'Leave it a few days, until she's back at home,' Brough suggested. 'She'll feel more like company then, and you know she's going to want to give your Harry a thorough interrogation…'

Laughter bubbled along the line.

'Yes. I've warned him about that already. Brough, we don't want a big wedding…just a quiet family ceremony. Harry says Christmas would be best for him because it fits in best with the farming calendar…'

'We'll talk about it when I get back,' Brough promised her, pausing before asking, 'What about Cox, Eve? Have you told *him* that—?'

'No, not yet,' Eve responded quickly. 'I know I'm going to have to but…' She paused. 'I…*we* wanted to tell you about us first…'

'Well, whatever you do, Eve,' Brough cautioned her, 'make sure you aren't on your own with him when you do tell him—or better still let me tell him for you.'

'No, Brough,' Eve told him gently. 'It's all right. Harry and I will handle this together.'

After he had terminated his call to his sister Brough took a deep breath and walked the length of the hospital car park whilst he assembled his thoughts. What he had just learned seemed nothing short of a small miracle, even if her Harry was rather an unexpected magician. He certainly seemed to have performed some very special magic in his sister's life, Brough recognised ruefully.

Although, technically, as Eve had just reminded him, she was legally an adult, he had always taken his brotherly responsibility towards her very seriously, and now, with one stroke, he was being freed, not just from that responsibility but also from the necessity of worrying about her emotional and financial future security, which meant...

Eagerly Brough reached for his mobile phone and punched in the number of Kelly's flat. Odd how easy it was to memorise certain vital numbers, how they seemed instinctively to lodge themselves in one's memory, he reflected wryly as he waited for Kelly to answer his call.

Five...ten minutes and three attempts later, he was forced to acknowledge that she must have gone out. He glanced at his watch. He wanted to have a further talk with the ward sister before she went off duty. He intended to spend the night in his grandmother's house just in case he should be needed urgently at her bedside. By the time he got there it would be too late to ring Kelly—she would no doubt be in bed and sound asleep—but first thing in the morning...

* * *

After she had replaced the telephone receiver following Brough's call, Eve turned to Harry, her eyes shining with love and relief.

'See, I *told* you he would understand,' Harry chided her lovingly.

'Yes, I know, but he was so…so stern and disapproving over Julian that I thought he'd be bound to think I couldn't possibly know my own mind when I told him I'd realised that I didn't love Julian at all and that you…'

She made a small happy sound beneath her breath as Harry put an end to her speech by kissing her very firmly and very determinedly. That was what she liked…*loved* about her Harry… He understood her so well…*knew* just how she felt…just what she wanted…knew that she was not like the majority of her peers in that she positively *wanted* someone to take control of her life and herself, that she adored having someone to stand beside her and protect her, to guide her masterfully.

But that someone had to be kind and gentle as well… He had to have the intuition and the love to know that the guiding hand she liked on the reins of her life had to be so delicately light that it could never chafe nor hurt her. Julian hadn't been like that. Julian had sometimes been very cruel to her, saying the most cutting and hurtful things…making her cry… Harry would never do that.

'You still have to tell Cox,' Harry reminded her quietly.

'I know,' Eve responded, 'but he frightens me a little, Harry… He keeps on telling me that he wants us to get engaged and he gets very angry when I tell him that Brough won't agree. He says it doesn't matter whether Brough agrees or not… I think he's more interested in my money than me,' Eve admitted in a small voice.

Privately, Harry thought so as well, and Cox was a

fool, in his opinion. He always had been, and not just a fool either, Harry reflected, his forehead creasing as he recalled certain things…certain old items of gossip he had picked up at home. But Harry was not the kind of person to pry into another person's personal life, and if Dee, his cousin, chose to place an embargo on certain events in her life, then he, for one, was quite happy to abide by it.

'Would you like *me* to tell him for you?' Harry suggested.

Immediately Eve's face lit up.

'Oh, Harry, would you…?'

Standing on tiptoe, she kissed him happily and then gave a small feminine gasp as he drew her closer and kissed her back, but much more deeply.

They were going to be so happy together, she and her Harry… She couldn't wait for the babies they were going to have, filling the old farmhouse with their presence and the love they would all share. All houses needed love and she certainly had plenty to give. She had already briefly met Harry's family, not officially as his intended bride because although she and Harry knew how strongly they felt about each other it had only been a *very* short time since they had first met, but she had seen from the looks his parents had exchanged that they had guessed how they felt about one another, and she had known straight away that she would get on well with them. Harry's mother was, in many ways, a younger version of her own grandmother, a plump, motherly woman who would draw her daughter-in-law safely beneath her maternal wing and keep her secure there.

'I'll go and see Cox first thing in the morning,' Harry promised her as he reluctantly released her.

'You could stay here tonight if you want,' Eve suggested daringly. 'Brough won't be coming back and...'

She stopped as she saw the stern look Harry was giving her.

'We agreed that we'd wait until we're married,' he reminded her.

Eve pouted and smiled.

'I know, but I love you so much and... Don't you want me, Harry...?'

The passion in the kiss he gave her was the only answer she needed.

'If I stay now, I'll have to make love to you, and if I do that... The Lawsons have a family tradition that the first child is born nine months virtually to the day of the wedding...I don't want our child to arrive ahead of that day,' he told her simply.

He had such pride, such moral fibre, such strength, Eve decided adoringly as she snuggled closer to him and whispered blissfully, 'Yes, Harry...'

Kelly came out of the darkness of a very deep sleep so abruptly that for a few seconds she was totally disorientated. Why was she alone in bed? Why...?

Frantically she sat up, searching the darkness of the room, and then the dim memory of Brough saying something to her about having to go came filtering back, clouded and fuzzy from the combined effects of the shock- and brandy-induced depth of her sleep.

Shakily she went to get herself a drink of water. Her throat felt dry and her eyes were scratchy and sore. In the cold pre-dawn chill of the kitchen she shivered a little as she stared into the darkness.

Had she and Brough really made love so intensely, so passionately, so poignantly? Had they really exchanged vows of love and commitment, told each other of the depth of their love for one another, or was it all simply a self-created fantasy...a dream? But no, she could feel the difference in her body, and knew that the words reverberating through her mind and her heart had been said...exchanged... Oh, Brough... A little weepily she started to tremble. Where on earth had he gone and why? If only she knew. Why *hadn't* he woken her up properly and spoken to her? Had he really meant what he had said to her, or...?

There was still so much they didn't really know about one another, despite the intimacy they had shared. So much he didn't know about *her*. She had tried to tell him about Julian...to explain...but her explanations had been swept away by the passion of the moment. What had he thought when he had walked in and discovered Julian with her like that?

Her thoughts began to chase one another around inside her head until she felt sick and dizzy with the weight of them, clasping her head in her hands as she protested aloud, 'No... No... Stop...'

It was too early for her to get up, and yet she knew if she went back to bed she wouldn't be able to sleep. After walking around her bedroom, touching the pillow where Brough's head had lain and then lifting it to her face to breathe in the scent of him and press the comfort of it close to her hot face, she reminded herself that she was a mature adult woman and that this type of fevered, frantic behaviour belonged more properly to early adolescence. Wearily she walked back into the sitting room, and then frowned as the things she had brought back from the Hartwell factory caught her eye.

Half an hour later she was blessedly engrossed in the records she was studying.

Now, the prospect of painting the new pieces for Brough's grandmother didn't just appeal to her artistically but emotionally as well. How typical of Brough, *her* Brough, that he should think of doing this, and typical too that he should search so assiduously to find someone, the *right* someone, to do the work for him.

How fitting…romantic even…that it should have been his quest to replace the missing pieces of a teaset which had originally been a wedding present for his grandmother that had brought them together, Kelly decided dreamily, determinedly ignoring the small, unwanted voice that insisted on reminding her that they had first met because of Julian Cox. That might have been their first meeting, but their *first mutual* realisation of their feelings for one another had been brought about by the Hartwell china, and when she told their grandchildren about it it would be that day together she would tell them about.

Their grandchildren.

A tiny shiver struck her. *Was* she taking too much for granted, reading too much into what Brough had said, the way he had held her…touched her…? When he had spoken of love had he merely been speaking of an emotion, a desire of the moment, and not meant it as she had done—that his feelings were so profound and deep that they were a commitment for life?

Suddenly her small doubts, tiny minnows nibbling at the sure structure of her belief in his love for her, had become a swarming shoal of destructive piranha eating greedily into and devouring her confidence.

Where was Brough? Why had he gone like that? She had a vague memory of him bending over her and speaking to her, but now, when it was crucially important to do so, she just couldn't remember what exactly it was he had said. Something about having to go…but why? Because once the immediate passion of the moment had been spent he had had second thoughts about loving her? Or had, perhaps, her declaration of love for him come too soon and, even worse, been unwanted? *Had* she assumed too much…*loved* too much?

Outside dawn was lightening the sky. Sternly she told herself that there was no point in allowing herself to think so destructively. Only Brough knew the answers to her questions. Only Brough could assuage her doubts. But where was he? She had his home telephone number; she could always ring him.

She looked at the telephone, her fingers itching to pick up the receiver and dial his number, but it was still only six o'clock in the morning. What if her worst fears were correct? What if he *had* regretted the intimacy they had shared? How would he react when he heard her voice, an unwanted intrusion into his privacy, and an even more unwanted reminder of something he might prefer to forget? And how would *she* feel, knowing that he didn't want to speak to her?

Give it time…give *him* time, she urged herself.

Six o'clock. Brough stretched and grimaced as he turned over in the small bed in his grandmother's spare bedroom. It was far too early to ring Kelly and too soon to leave for home. He wanted to check with the specialist that his grandmother was truly on the way to recovery before he did that, and they had told him at the hospital last night that he couldn't see the specialist until ten o'clock in the morning.

He would ring Kelly before he left the hospital to come home, he comforted himself. God, but he missed her…wanted her. He frowned as he remembered the look of fear and revulsion on her face as Julian Cox held her. There was something that just didn't jell, that just didn't ring true to her character about her whole relationship with Cox—something he could sense without being able to analyse properly. It was obvious that she loathed him, but at the ball she had been actively flirting with him.

Brough frowned.

'We're old friends,' she had told him dismissively when he had challenged her, her whole attitude towards him almost aggressive. In a way that an animal was aggressive when it tried to cover up its fear?

Brough knew with a gut-deep instinct that there was no way Kelly, *his* Kelly, could *ever* have done anything so directly opposed to her open, straightforward nature as to be deceitful. It simply wasn't her. And neither would he have thought it would have been her ever to be even remotely attracted to a man like Julian Cox. It wasn't his own male ego or vanity that made him think that. He simply knew that she was too sensitive, too aware, too intelligent to be attracted by a man who held her sex in such obvious contempt.

But maybe, just maybe, it *was* possible that a much younger and more impressionable and vulnerable Kelly might have been unable to see through the façade that Cox was so adept at throwing around himself. His own sister, after all, had fallen for it, but that didn't explain why Kelly had been flirting so heavily with Cox on the night of the ball.

Wide awake now, Brough closed his eyes and tried to collect his thoughts. What was he doing? Whatever may or may not have happened in Kelly's past, it *was* her past. She had no need to make any explanations or apologies for it to him. He loved her as she was and for what she was, and if she *had* made an error of judgement...

An error of judgement? By allowing Cox to be her lover? The vicious kick of emotion he could feel in his stomach was an all-male gut reaction, but just as immediate and even more powerful was an instinctive awareness that there was no way Kelly would ever have shared that kind of intimacy with Julian Cox. Brough had no idea how he knew that...he just knew it. And, knowing it, he owed it to her and to their love to allow her privacy over the whole issue of just what role Julian Cox had played in her life prior to their meeting.

Whatever it may or may not have been, there was one thing Brough was one hundred per cent sure of: it most certainly didn't give Cox the right to behave towards her in the way he had been doing, half frightening the life out of her, bullying her.

Suddenly Brough was even more anxious to get back to her. Half past six... He was sorely tempted to ring her, but the things he wanted to say to her were so intensely personal that they simply could not be said over the phone.

Eve had told him that she and Harry wanted a Christmas wedding. Well, they could most certainly have it, but his own marriage to Kelly was going to take place first. Well, so far as he was concerned it was. Kelly, he suspected, might take a bit of persuading. She took her responsibilities to her partner, Beth, very seriously; that much was obvious.

Six forty-five. Brough groaned, quickly calculating how long it was going to be before he could get back to Rye-on-Averton and to Kelly.

'Are you awake?' Eve whispered softly to Harry.

Sternly he sat up in bed and looked at her. She might

have been able to persuade him that he should stay over-
night with her, but he had been very firmly determined
that they would sleep in separate rooms, and they had.
Eve was so sweetly naive that she had no idea of just
what she was doing to his self-control, curling up at the
bottom of his bed like that in her soft white nightdress,
her long hair flowing down her back.

'What are you doing in here?' he demanded.

'I came to talk to you...I couldn't sleep,' she answered, whispering excitedly, 'Oh, Harry, I'm so
happy...' Her face suddenly clouded. 'When are you
going to see Julian?'

'Nine o'clock,' Harry responded promptly, 'and then
you and I are going out to celebrate.'

As she looked down at her bare left hand he followed
her line of thought and told her gruffly, 'I've got my
grandmother's ring... I'd like you to have it, but if you
don't like it...'

'Oh, I'm sure I shall,' Eve breathed, pink-cheeked.
'Oh, Harry,' she repeated, flinging herself into his arms,
'I'm so excited. I still can't quite believe what's hap-
pening...'

Seven o'clock. Dee pushed back the duvet and padded
over to her bedroom window. Beyond it she could see
the soft rolling countryside, the fertile acres which had
been tended by her ancestors for so many generations.

Once, those ancestors had been as fertile as the fields
they tilled, but she and Harry were the only descendants
in their generation, a poor crop yield indeed. Harry
would marry, of course, and hopefully would produce
sons and daughters to continue the family tradition. She
would never marry nor have children since through her

own experience as a motherless girl she had formed very strong views on the need of a child to have the loving support of both its parents. An old-fashioned view in this day and age, perhaps, but it was hers and she had the right to have it—just as she had the right to choose whether or not to yield to the demand of her own fast-ticking biological clock.

Yes, the future of their family was solely dependent on Harry. It needn't have been that way. There had once been a time when... But what was the point in dwelling on that now? Unbidden she had a sharp mental image of Julian Cox. Her whole body stiffened as a surge of pain gripped her.

She had waited for such a long time for the chance to punish Julian Cox for what he had done...to punish him in a way which would ensure that he suffered just as she had suffered...but once again it seemed that he was evading that justice, escaping it. There was no point in her being angry with Kelly. Love was a powerfully potent force. No one knew that better than she, but it wasn't over yet; there was still Anna's role to be played. Julian still needed money and he needed it desperately now. Brough had already refused to invest any money with him, thus closing down that avenue of escape to him. But Julian could still marry Eve and thereby gain access to her money.

But Brough was his sister's trustee, and once Kelly told him what Julian had done to Beth it was Dee's guess that Brough would never allow Julian to marry his sister. Julian was in debt up to his neck and sinking fast...very fast...

So maybe everything wasn't lost after all. Julian might have been clever enough technically not to break the law, but he had certainly come very close to doing so.

Through the people she had hired, Dee had discovered a vast hidden tangle of false names and hideaway companies, all of which could be linked to him if, like her, you used a little creative thinking. He might deceive others but he couldn't deceive her. There were the aliases with the same initials as his, the clever use of his mother's maiden name and the names of people now dead.

No, legally he might be able to laugh in the faces of his victims as he challenged them to claim restitution from him, but morally— But what did Julian know of morals? What did he care about the good name of others, about their pride in it, their shame at losing it? Nothing.

A bitter smile curled her mouth as her eyes closed on a wave of sharp pain.

Her father had been such a proud man. Distant and old-fashioned towards her in many ways, perhaps, but always, always scrupulously honest in everything he did...*everything*. But he was dead now, and it was pointless to dwell on how much closer they might have become once they had been able to meet as adults. That chance was gone, destroyed...like her option to marry and have children; stolen from her...

Stop it, you're getting maudlin, she warned herself sharply. It was time for her to get up. She had work to do. The markets in Hong Kong would soon be closing. She had investments there she needed to check on.

Julian enjoyed gambling on the futures market. Or at least he had done until recently, when he had begun to sustain such heavy losses, outsmarted and outbid, outbought and outsold by a shadowy rival who seemed to second-guess his every thought. Poor Julian!

When he woke up this morning it would be to find

that his investments had sunk without trace, that the profit he had been so in need of making had become a loss.

Suddenly Dee began to feel better.

CHAPTER TEN

WHITE-FACED, Julian stared at the screen of his computer, a sick feeling of shock and disbelief coagulating his blood.

He had woken up two hours ago, his tongue thick with yesterday's alcohol and his head throbbing. That bitch Kelly thought she was so clever; leading him on and then dropping him, but he'd get even with her. But first that hot tip he had picked up yesterday from his informer had sounded such a sure thing. He had bought heavily into it, using all his last reserves, but this morning when he had gone to check the market he had hardly been able to believe his eyes. The stock was gone, wiped out, finished, and with it everything he owned. *Everything*.

He pushed the computer screen off his desk with such violence that it hit the floor. He picked up the keyboard and flung it against the wall of his office in an attempt to relieve his panic and fury. What the hell was he going to do? He *had* to have money by the end of this month. He *had* to. And it wasn't just a matter of the banks calling in his loans and stopping him trading.

A long time ago Julian had hit on and discovered how easy it was to persuade gullible and often naively managed small private charities to accept his offer of free investment advice. Eagerly they had accepted, co-opting him onto their boards, offering him access to their monies, only too glad to have him remove from their shoulders the burden of managing their investments. Just so long as he provided them with an income which increased from year to year they were happy and didn't enquire about their capital...

And that was exactly what he had done...until now... Never mind the fact that their capital was long since gone, used to fund his own lavish lifestyle, used to make investments so perilously on the outside of mere risky that no one else would touch them; just the excitement he had got from backing these outsiders had given him more of a buzz than sex and even drugs ever had.

Of course, the empty coffers of some of those early and rather clumsy siphoning-offs of funds had quickly come to light, but luckily he had been able to place the blame elsewhere and convince people that *he* was not the one responsible for the foolish investment and subsequent loss of their money, and he had even had the signatures of his co-investors to prove it. He had always been rather good at forging other people's signatures. The first time he had put his skill to a financial advantage had been when he had stolen a 'friend's' cheque book.

Those had been good days; fortune had favoured him and his investments and it had been no problem to move money from one place to another as and when it was needed. But now things were different. The markets were running against him and he had made heavy losses...too heavy... He needed money and he needed it urgently. It was all Kelly's fault. He had gambled heavily on being able to persuade her to allow him to advise her, on how best to 'invest' her inheritance. But now she had dropped him—made a fool of him—and no woman did that.

It was a pity that Eve didn't have access to her capital, and Brough certainly wasn't going to be easy to persuade to allow her to have full control over it; but still, it was better than nothing.

The sweat of fear that had soaked his skin was begin-

ning to disappear and, with it, his earlier panic. He was
worrying too much and too soon. What he needed was
something to calm him down, help him relax…a drink…

He went to find the bottle of gin he had discarded in
the kitchen the previous evening and then stopped as he
heard his doorbell ring.

It was just gone nine o'clock.

It had been well gone ten o'clock when Brough had seen
the specialist, who had declared very reassuringly that
his grandmother would make a full recovery, and then
Brough had gone from his office to his grandmother's
bed to spend his allocated fifteen minutes with her. Kelly
would be in the shop by now. Hurrying outside the hospital, he reached for his mobile phone.

Kelly had just opened the post when she heard the
phone ring. As she reached for the receiver her heart
started to beat very fast, her face flushing a soft pink,
but to her disappointment her caller wasn't Brough but
Beth.

'Hi… How are you?' her friend and partner asked her.

'I'm fine; how are you?' Kelly returned automatically.

'Not so good,' Beth responded. 'I'm still trying to fix
up a visit to that factory I told you about.'

As Kelly listened to her friend's enthusiastic voice she
suddenly heard the sound that warned her that a second
caller was trying to get through on her line. Was it
Brough? Even if it was, she could hardly cut Beth off
in mid-sentence, she acknowledged frustratedly as her
friend paused for a brief breath before continuing, 'Look,
the reason I'm ringing is that I've decided I'm going to
stay on in Prague for some more time. It could take me
a while to track down this factory, and I'm determined
to do it, Kelly, even if I have to learn the language to
make myself understood,' she told her friend with un-

usual fierceness. 'I don't care how much Alex tries to put me off... I *want* that glass. Look, I'm intending to move into a cheaper hotel for the rest of my stay, but I don't know which one yet. I'll give you a ring once I've sorted something out.'

'Oh, Beth, you will take care, won't you?' Kelly begged her. 'If your interpreter doesn't think it's wise—'

'He's just being awkward and difficult,' Beth assured her firmly. 'I'm an adult, Kelly, not a child,' she added with un-Beth-like grittiness, saying before Kelly could raise any further objections, 'Look, I have to go; I'll be in touch. Bye...'

Frowning a little, Kelly replaced the receiver. Beth was obviously determined to track down this elusive factory, but her determination seemed so at odds with her normal gentle, almost passive behaviour that Kelly was a little puzzled by it. She certainly seemed to thoroughly dislike her interpreter, who, from what she had said, seemed to be doing his best to be extraordinarily obstructive.

Nervously Kelly dialled the numbers that would allow her to check her answering service.

Her heart started to thump as the recorded voice announced that she had one message.

'Hear message?' the tinny voice asked.

'Yes,' Kelly whispered, her throat suddenly constricted.

'Kelly, it's me, Brough. I need to talk to you...see you... I should be home around eleven-thirty; could you possibly call round? I'd come to the shop, but what I want to say I'd prefer to say in private... Bye now.'

'Repeat?' the tinny recording was demanding rather bossily. 'Repeat?'

'No. No...' Kelly responded automatically.

What did Brough mean? What *was* it he wanted to

say to her? Her mouth had gone dry and her heart was thudding heavily in a drumbeat of doom.

He *had* changed his mind, made a mistake… That was what he wanted to say to her and *that* was why he wanted privacy in order to do so. He *didn't* really love her at all.

Kelly started to shiver, causing the customer who had just walked into the shop to exclaim sympathetically, 'Oh, my, you do look poorly! It's not this virus that's been going round, is it? I should go straight to bed if I were you.'

If only the cause of her pain *were* merely a virus, Kelly reflected after her customer had gone. What time was it now? Eleven-thirty, Brough had said, his voice sounding remote and grave. He wouldn't have asked her to go round…

She would have to close the shop; it was too late to get someone in to take over from her. It would be the earliest lunch hour in history, she decided miserably. There was no point in trying to deceive herself or give herself false hope. Brough was only confirming what she herself had been thinking. He had had second thoughts, realised that her feelings were much, much stronger than his, and now he wanted to make the situation completely clear to her. That was the way he was. He wasn't the kind of man simply to walk away without any explanation.

He was sorry, he would tell her. He didn't want to hurt her. What they had had had been good…very good…but for him it had simply been a one-off and not, as she had obviously believed, the basis, the foundation, for a lasting relationship or a permanent commitment.

Five past eleven… She would leave at eleven-fifteen… Plenty of time for her to drive to where Brough was living. She reached mechanically for a cloth so that she could pass the time in polishing some of the items they had on display, but her hands were shaking so much she put it down again. In her present state of agitation she was likely to do more harm than good.

Julian stared drunkenly at the screen of his computer which he had picked up off the floor. His system had crashed…just like the whole of his life. The last thing he had expected when he'd opened the door to his caller two hours ago had been to discover Harry standing on his doorstep. The other man had asked him quietly if he could come in. Automatically, Julian had agreed.

'There's something I have to tell you,' Harry began calmly as Julian led him into his untidy, dusty sitting room, shaking his head when Julian offered him a drink, saying mildly, 'Rather too early for me…'

'It's never too early…' Julian responded boastfully as he poured himself another gin.

He had no idea what Harry wanted. He only knew the other man vaguely and totally despised him. Harry represented everything that he himself loathed.

'Eve has asked me to come and see you,' Harry began quietly. 'She and I are getting married…'

Julian stared at him in disbelief. Was he trying to play some kind of joke on him? He searched the other man's face, a slow sensation of sick realisation creeping like death along his veins. This was no joke.

'What the hell are you saying? She's marrying *me*,' Julian told him furiously.

Harry said nothing but just continued to look steadily at him.

'No! No! I don't believe it,' Julian insisted, starting to shake his head, trying to dispel the clouds of panic swamping him. 'I want to see her…talk to her…'

'I'm sorry, but I don't think that would be a good idea,' Harry told him politely.

'*You* don't think...?' Julian gave him an ugly look. 'Eve is *my* girlfriend. We're all but engaged, dammit, and—'

'She *was* your girlfriend,' Harry agreed quietly, 'although...' He stopped and gave Julian a steady look. 'It seems to me that you rather took her for granted. Perhaps if you'd valued her a little more...as she deserves to be valued...'

'Oh, my God, now I've heard it all—*you* telling *me* how to treat a woman...' Julian gave him a contemptuous look and tossed back the last of his drink. 'What the hell do *you* know about women? Nothing...' he jeered. 'She loves *me*; she told me so... She's besotted with me...' he boasted.

Harry said nothing, refusing to retaliate, simply watching him with a look in his eyes that goaded Julian into walking unsteadily across the floor and pouring himself another drink.

'You can't do this to me...and don't think I don't know who's behind it. It's that precious brother of hers; he never wanted—'

'This has nothing to do with Brough,' Harry corrected him. 'Eve and I are in love...'

'Eve in love...with you? Don't make me laugh. She loves *me*.'

She did love him. She had told him so in a soft, nervous little voice, her eyes big with wonder and excitement. It had been so easy to trick her into believing he had fallen for her. She was so trusting... She hadn't even questioned the fact that he hadn't taken her to bed.

'I respect you too much,' he had told her untruthfully.

The truth was that his drinking and the intense pressure of his lifestyle meant that sex was the last thing on his mind, the last desire he had. It took a woman like Kelly to arouse *that* need in him, not a babyish innocent like Eve.

Julian *knew* that it was her brother who was behind her decision to drop him. Brough had guessed that Julian was after her money, of course. Julian gave a small mental shrug. So what? He didn't give a damn what Brough had or hadn't guessed, and as for preferring Harry to him... That was ridiculous...impossible...

'I don't believe you... I'm going to see Eve—talk to her,' he announced, walking unsteadily towards the door, but oddly, when he got there, Harry was standing in front of it, barring his way.

'No, I'm sorry, but you're not,' Harry told him calmly.

Julian looked drunkenly at him.

'What is this? You can't stop me...'

Harry stood solidly in front of the door, simply looking at him. A little to his own surprise Julian discovered that he was actually backing off. What the hell was he doing? He wasn't afraid of Harry.

'I think you'll find it would be best for everyone concerned if you simply accept the situation,' he heard Harry saying gently to him, to his utter amazement.

'People will soon forget. After all, it isn't as though you were actually engaged, and neither Eve nor I shall say anything. People will simply believe that the two of you drifted apart. It happens all the time.'

Julian swayed and focused vacantly on Harry's face. What the hell was he trying to suggest? That he, Julian Cox, was in danger of being humiliated by people thinking that Eve had dropped him? No way!

'Eve mentioned that you have business interests in Hong Kong. I've heard it is a fascinating part of the world, even more so these days... Have you ever been there? I haven't myself... Farming doesn't combine well with travelling...'

Julian continued to gape at him.

Was Harry actually daring subtly to suggest to him, to *warn* him, that he should leave town...? No, it was impossible. Harry simply wasn't like that. He didn't have the nerve...nor the subtlety. No, he was imagining it, Julian assured himself. The other man was too unworldly to know that there was no way Julian could visit Hong Kong right now, not with the money he owed out there, the enemies he had made.

'I'll let myself out,' he heard Harry saying mildly. When he reached the front door, Harry turned to him and commented quietly, 'I should keep off the drink for a while if I were you.' Then he turned round and opened the door to leave.

Now as he sat staring blindly at the screen in front of him, Julian couldn't believe it. His life was in chaos, *ruins*... He had been counting on Eve and her inheritance. By God, but she wasn't going to do this to him. No way... He could soon make her change her mind.

He needed a drink. He lurched over to the kitchen worktop, frowning impatiently when he saw the empty bottle. Well, he would just have to go out and buy some more, wouldn't he? He still had enough money for that...he could still afford to buy himself a *drink*...to get drunk... By God, yes, he could still afford to do that, and once he had...

As Julian opened his front door the brilliance of the bright morning hit his eyeballs in fiery darts of pain. Oblivious to the looks on the faces of other pedestrians, he started to stagger towards the centre of the town. His car was parked outside the house, but some vestige of self-preservation warned him that it would be extremely unwise for him to drive.

Kelly too had made the same decision, but for very different reasons. It wasn't drink that made her aware that her reactions were simply not good enough for her to drive anywhere safely. She was trembling from head to foot as she opened the shop door, dreading her coming interview with Brough, and yet knowing that she was too proud to ring him up and simply tell him that it wasn't necessary for him to say anything; that she had already guessed what he wanted to tell her and that she understood.

Pride, was it? Was she *sure* it wasn't more of a desperate, anguished yearning on the part of a woman far too deeply and vulnerably in love to deny herself the masochistic pleasure of spending some last precious minutes with the man she loved?

It seemed to be adding an even finer edge of cruelty to her unhappiness that it should be such a wonderful day, the sun shining, the air soft and fresh, people walking about dressed in light clothes, smiling...

As she turned the corner at the bottom of the street she could see across the town square to the river, glinting happily in the sunshine. Rye-on-Averton was such a pretty town that normally just to walk through it lifted her spirits, but not today—no, definitely not today.

Head down, fighting to hold back the tears threatening to overwhelm her, Kelly walked quickly to Brough's house.

She was less than five yards away from it when she suddenly heard someone calling her name. Lifting her head, she froze as she recognised Julian Cox staggering towards her from the opposite direction. He was quite obviously drunk and looked totally repulsive, she decided as she saw his stubbly jaw and creased clothes.

'Kelly... What are you doing here...or can I guess? Come crawling round after Brough, have you? What happened? Dropped you, has he?' he tormented her jeer-ingly. 'Well, what did you expect? Surely you aren't really stupid enough not to guess what he was up to? He wanted to draw you off me because of his sister. That was all... Didn't you guess? Surely you must have realised that a man like him would *never* look seriously at someone like you, someone who's been to bed with half the town... Not that he minded getting a taste of what you've got to offer himself... He told me that...said he might as well have full value for his money...'

Julian had gone straight from his house to the super-market, where he had discovered, contrary to his belief, he did *not* have enough money on him to buy any al-cohol. Infuriated, both by this and Harry's interview with him, he had, instead of going home, headed for Brough's house, intending to try to persuade Eve to see reason and change her mind. She would more than likely be on her own at this time of day and he was pretty sure he could persuade her to listen to him.

But just as he had reached the house he had seen Kelly approaching it from the opposite direction, and imme-diately he had remembered just how she had rejected him and how, because of that rejection, Brough Frobisher had humiliated him—and, no doubt, brought pressure to bear on Eve to end their relationship.

All the fury and vindictiveness caused by this sud-denly found a target in Kelly. What better way of getting back at Brough than by destroying his relationship with Kelly? If he knew anything about women—and he did—she would never stay if he told her that Brough had discussed her sexually with someone else.

Now, looking at her face, he knew he had been right—God, he was enjoying hurting her, making her pay for rejecting him.

'Did you really think he wanted you?' he taunted her cruelly. 'How could he? He saw the way you were all over *me* at the ball... He's a proud man, our Brough...far too proud to want *my* leavings...'

Brough had not made as good time coming back as he had hoped. Some unexpected road works had held him up and then, to make matters worse, he hadn't been able to park his car outside his house but had had to leave it much further down the street.

It was already gone half past eleven. Quickening his stride, he turned the corner to see Kelly standing outside the house with her back to him, facing Julian Cox. What the hell was he doing...?

Immediately Brough started to run.

Julian, who was facing him, saw him first, smirking triumphantly at him as he reached them, taunting Brough drunkenly, 'How did it feel having my leavings?' He waved his arms towards Kelly. 'She's pretty good, I know, but just in case you're interested I can recommend someone even better... They say that an enthusiastic amateur is better than a professional any day, I know, but...'

Kelly made a small, tortured whimper of protest but both men seemed to be ignoring her.

'Well, you saw for yourself at the ball how it was,' Julian continued tauntingly. He was beginning to enjoy himself now. The effects of the drink he had consumed earlier were beginning to wear off, sharpening his instincts. Kelly looked white and sick. Oh, yes, he really was enjoying this.

'Of course, Kelly and I are old mates. She and I had a little thing going when I was dating her partner, Beth. Kelly's like that. She *prefers* a man who belongs to another woman, don't you, my pet? She says it adds to the enjoyment…gives it an extra kick of excitement for her…and she certainly likes her excitement, does our Kelly. Has she…?' He used a phrase which horrified Kelly and made her face burn with shame. She couldn't bring herself to look at Brough. How could she defend herself against Julian's charges without going into lengthy explanations? And besides, what was the point? She already knew that Brough didn't want her, didn't *love* her as she did him.

Not returning her love was one thing, she reminded herself in anguish, but having him receive this kind of information about her, knowing how it *must* affect his judgement of her and his future memories of her, was quite another.

'It's okay, though,' Julian continued laconically. 'I've put her in the picture about Eve and she knows that you were just using her to draw… All you really wanted was to get her out of my life… Is…she in, by the way? I promised her I'd take her out this morning to choose an engagement ring.'

As he spoke Julian stepped determinedly past Kelly, almost knocking her over.

'I agree with what you said about her,' he commented loudly to Brough. 'She's really just a good one-night lay.'

Suddenly, as Julian looked into Brough's eyes, the drunken fumes momentarily cleared from his brain. He had, he recognised sickly, made a bad mistake—a dangerous error of judgement. But it was too late for him to have second thoughts now, he realised as the contempt in Brough's eyes became a seething fury.

Kelly couldn't bear to hear any more. Without turning to look at Brough she started to walk and then to run desperately away, ignoring the concerned stares of passers-by as she ran, head down, along the street, back in the direction she had come.

Brough watched her like someone turned to stone.

'I need to see Eve, Brough,' Julian started to plead whiningly.

Cold-eyed, Brough turned to look at him. 'Eve is marrying Harry,' he told him. 'You're not wanted here, Cox, and if I find you *anywhere* near my sister for *any* reason...'

'Are you threatening me?' Julian began to bluster as he knew he had gone too far in venting his rage against Kelly.

'No. I'm *telling* you,' Brough said softly. 'And, by the way, you've wasted your time coming here. Eve isn't here; she's gone to visit her in-laws-to-be. Now, if you'll excuse me I—'

'I wouldn't waste your time going after Kelly,' Julian interrupted him, grinning. 'Everything I said about her was true. But you must have found out what she's like for yourself by now. She doesn't make a man waste time; I'll give her that. Pretty energetic in bed, isn't she? Pity she's not been a bit more exclusive about how she hands it out...'

Julian never saw the blow that hit him, he certainly felt it, though, as he dropped to the floor, trying to stem the blood pouring from his nose. He started to curse but Brough had already gone.

Instinctively Kelly headed for the river path and its protective seclusion.

She *couldn't* go back to the shop, not just yet, and there was nowhere else, no *one* else, she could go to— not like this...

Oh, but it had hurt, hurt more than anything else in her life, knowing what Brough must be thinking about her. None of Julian's crude accusations were true, of course—at least not in the way *he* had said them.

Apart from a brief, immature adolescent relationship with the boy who had been her first lover, there had been no one else in her life other than Brough, and certainly no one else in her bed. But how on earth could she prove that to Brough?

He might not love her but at least he had liked her, *respected* her, and she couldn't bear to think of him now carrying an image of her that Julian had painted for him. But even if she could bring herself to face him and explain, why *should* he believe her?

The river path was empty of other walkers, and Kelly's fast pace had slowed as the thoughts started to tumble around in her head.

'Kelly!'

The shock of hearing Brough's voice behind her made her stumble, but immediately he was beside her, catching her up in his arms.

'*Why* did you run off like that?' he demanded as her body stiffened defensively in his hold.

Agitatedly Kelly shook her head. The shock of him suddenly appearing, never mind what being held so close to him was doing to her nervous system, was too much for her to cope with.

'Those things that Julian said—it wasn't...I never... You have been the only one—' Kelly stopped, unable to go on.

She could feel Brough's tension, and when he lifted his hand to raise her chin so that she was forced to look into his eyes Kelly felt as though she would die from the pain of what she was expecting him to say, but to her shock what she saw in his eyes wasn't contempt and rejection, but love and tenderness and, along with it, anxiety.

'Kelly, I don't understand. You surely don't think I could *possibly* place any credence on what Cox was saying?'

Kelly stared at him.

'You didn't…you don't believe him?' she whispered.

'Of course not. How could I? What kind of man do you think I am?' he demanded, his expression changing, darkening. 'I certainly don't need a man like Cox to tell me *anything* about the woman I love. I can learn about her for myself, and what I have learned…'

The woman he *loved*. Kelly felt as though her heart was going to burst with joy.

'You *love* me?' she asked him huskily.

He was still frowning.

'Of course I do. You *know* that. I told you… Kelly… Kelly, darling, please don't cry,' he begged her as he drew her closer. 'Please, please don't cry, my love…'

'You *left* me,' Kelly wept, more out of relief and joy than unhappiness; after all, what possible reason was there for her to be unhappy *now*, with Brough's arms around her, Brough's words of love ringing so sweetly in her ears, Brough's lips so close to hers?

'I *had* to,' Brough told her. 'I'd had a phone call to say that my grandmother had been taken into hospital. You were so deeply asleep I couldn't bear to waken you…'

'Your *grandmother*,' Kelly repeated, instantly asking anxiously, 'Oh, Brough, what…? How…?'

'She's fine… She had a fall followed by pneumonia but she's well on the way to recovery now and very much looking forward to meeting you.'

'You've told her about me?' Kelly asked him shyly. 'Oh, what…?'

'I told her you were interested in seeing her teaset,'

Brough teased her, relenting when he saw the uncertainty still clouding her eyes.

'I told her I love you and that I want you to be my wife,' he told her huskily. 'She can't wait to meet you and I've promised that I'll do my best to persuade you to come with me when I drive down to see her tomorrow…'

'Oh, Brough…'

'You're crying again,' he chided her.

'It's because I'm so happy,' Kelly assured him. 'Say that again…'

'What, that you're crying?'

'No…what you said about loving me and wanting to marry me,' Kelly told him softly.

'I love you and I want you to marry me,' Brough repeated dutifully, but before Kelly could respond to him he was cupping her face and kissing her tenderly and slowly, and then not tenderly at all as her emotions caught fire and she clung passionately to him, returning the demanding pressure of his mouth, her whole body singing with joy as it recognised just how much he truly loved and wanted her.

'Brough, about Julian…' Kelly began slowly when she had finally managed to persuade him to stop kissing her.

'What about him? He means nothing to us; he has no place in our lives, our future,' Brough pointed out.

'No. But, yes, he does have a place…sort of…in *my* past,' Kelly told him carefully, adding hastily, 'Oh, no, it's not that we were ever lovers.' She gave a small shudder. 'I couldn't…he's loathsome…and I… Well, as a matter of fact, you've been the only…that is… There was a boy when… Brough, how can I explain about Julian if you keep on kissing me?' she protested shakily.

'You don't have to tell me anything about your past,' Brough told her quietly.

'You are the person you are, Kelly, and that includes everything and everyone in your past that has gone to make up that person, that Kelly—*my* Kelly. Without those experiences you wouldn't be the Kelly I love so much... You didn't really think I'd place any credence on those ridiculous lies that Cox was telling, did you?' he asked her, obviously pained that she might have done.

'I... I...I thought, after the way you left me, that you'd had second thoughts about...about us. And then, when I got your telephone message, I thought you wanted to see me to tell me that...that it was...that I was...that there wasn't any future for us...'

Kelly bit her lip as she heard the incredulous sound he made, but she was determined to finish what she had to say.

'I...' She raised her head and looked him firmly in the eye. 'When you and I met at that ball, I *was* flirting with Julian, and it was because of that that I thought you might think...'

'What I thought that night was that even though I knew nothing at all about you there was something odd about your behaviour, something that somehow didn't ring quite true, something alien and quite patently uncomfortable for you in your behaviour towards Cox.'

'You felt all that but...but you kissed me as though—' Kelly began, but Brough stopped her.

'That was an experiment,' he told her boldly. 'I was curious about you, about the...er...discrepancies in your behaviour and the person I sensed you were, and I was curious about... I felt that if I kissed you I would immediately be able to tell—'

'You're fibbing,' Kelly interrupted him. 'How could you tell anything from just one kiss?'

'I could tell that I was falling in love with you,' Brough told her wryly, silencing her before continuing, 'It did puzzle me that you should be acting in a way that was quite plainly out of character for you,' he admitted quietly. 'But I decided that whatever your reasons for doing so, they were *your* reasons. You are a woman, adult, mature, perfectly capable of making your own decisions and doing whatever you decide is right for you. I have no right nor reason to question those decisions, nor would I want to do so,' he told her gravely. 'As I've already told you, Kelly, I love the person you *are*, and whatever you choose to do or not to do...'

'I did it for Beth,' Kelly told him quickly. 'It was Dee's idea...'

Briefly she explained what they had planned to do.

'Beth... So that was the girl Cox was seeing before he met Eve. Cox told Eve that she was obsessed with him and that—'

'No way...' Kelly told him indignantly. '*He* was on the verge of getting engaged to Beth when he met Eve and then he told poor Beth that she had imagined everything...that he had never said he wanted to marry her. But Beth's not like that. She's gentle and sweet, a passive, loving...'

'Rather like my sister, in fact,' Brough concluded grimly.

'A little like that,' Kelly agreed. 'But of course Beth didn't have any money...' She sighed. 'I'm sorry if I sounded unkind...'

'No, you're only corroborating my own thoughts,' Brough told her. 'However, fortunately that's not a problem we need to worry about any more, since Eve has informed me that she is in love with Harry and that they intend to get married at Christmas. Christmas, apparently, is a perfect time for a marriage in the farming community…'

'Harry…? I knew he was attracted to her,' Kelly admitted. 'He's Dee's cousin. That was why he was escorting me at the ball.

'Brough, what are you doing?' she demanded as Brough turned her round and, tucking her into his side, proceeded to walk briskly back in the direction they had just come.

'I'm taking you home with me,' he told her firmly, and then added huskily, 'Do you realise it's almost twenty-four hours since I made love with you?'

'Brough,' Kelly protested as he took her back in his arms and proceeded to show her just how long a time he felt those hours had been.

'Kelly…' he teased her softly as he nibbled at her bottom lip and felt the sweet response of her body and herself to his caresses.

'I've got to go back and re-open the shop,' she told him.

'Why?' Brough demanded. 'There's no point; all its stock has just been sold.'

'What…what are you talking about?' Kelly demanded in bemusement. 'Who…? What…?'

'I'm talking about the fact that if the only way I can get you to myself is to buy every piece of stock in your precious shop, then that's exactly what I shall do,' Brough told her rawly.

'You can't do that,' Kelly protested. 'It will cost you a fortune…'

'Yes, I can. I'm a very rich man,' Brough assured her sweetly, adding huskily, 'The richest and happiest man in the world now I've got you, my love, my precious only one true love.

'My grandmother's already nagging me about a white wedding.'

'Cream...' Kelly murmured, nuzzling closer to the promising intoxication of his mouth. 'Cream suits me better...'

'Mmm... Well, there's no way I intend to wait until Eve gets married...'

Kelly's heart gave a funny little jump.

'It takes at least three weeks for the banns to be read, and my family will have to come back from South Africa...'

'Mmm... Well, that certainly won't take three weeks, but I hear what you're saying. How about we make it the same time as Nan's wedding anniversary, which is several weeks away? I know it would mean a lot to her if you and I chose the same wedding day...'

'It sounds perfect,' Kelly told him happily.

'It *is* perfect...like you...perfect in every way...and don't you ever forget it,' Brough told her huskily as he drew her even more deeply into his arms.

EPILOGUE

'TRY not to feel too bad that things didn't work out,' Anna tried to console Dee gently. 'We may not have been able to reveal Julian in his true colours, but at least Beth seems to be getting over him. She never mentioned him once the last time she rang me, and in fact she seemed far more concerned about the problems this interpreter's causing her than her broken engagement. And just think, if it hadn't been for *you*, Kelly and Brough might never have met...'

Dee gave her a rueful look.

They were sitting in the pretty conservatory at the back of Anna's house, Anna's cat purring loudly on her knee whilst her little dog begged hopefully for crumbs of the home-made biscuit Dee was eating.

'I wish I could be more like you, Anna,' Dee told her in a rare admission of self-criticism. 'You have such a peaceful acceptance of life...'

'Maybe now,' Anna agreed with her gentle smile, 'but not always. When I first lost Ralph, my husband...' She paused and shook her head. 'But that's all in the past now.' She looked thoughtfully at Dee before continuing quietly, 'Have you ever thought, Dee, that it might be time for *you* to put Julian and whatever...?' She stopped and bit her lip as she saw the storm clouds beginning to darken Dee's magnificent eyes.

'No. Never. There's no way I can put Julian in the past until—'

Abruptly Dee stopped. Close though she had become to both Kelly and Anna these last few weeks, there were still some things she just couldn't bring herself to discuss with them, some confidences she couldn't even make to gentle, understanding Anna.

'It isn't over yet,' she said fiercely instead, reminding Anna, 'At least he's taking the bait in *our* trap.'

Their trap? Wisely Anna said nothing. Something that went far, far deeper into Dee's past than her relatively recent friendship with her own goddaughter, Beth, was motivating Dee in her need to see Julian get his just deserts.

'Julian's already made overtures to you, hinting that he could put you in the way of a highly profitable investment opportunity, hasn't he?'

'Yes, he has,' Anna agreed.

'Excellent. We'll get him yet, and when we do...'

'When we do, what?' Anna pressed her gently.

Dee turned to her, her eyes bleak with an anguished pain that touched Anna's tender heart as she told her grimly, 'When we do, we'll expose him for the liar and the cheat that he is! The liar, the cheat and the murderer,' Dee emphasised.

The *murderer*? Anna was too shocked to say anything, and Dee was already getting up, pausing only to give the waiting dog the titbit she had saved for him before turning to hug Anna and tell her, 'I'll be in touch. There are a few arrangements I need to make to ensure that you'll have sufficient cash available to properly tempt Julian. I think probably that fifty thousand pounds should do it...'

'Fifty thousand pounds!' Anna gasped in protest. 'Oh, Dee, so much. But...'

'It's nothing,' Dee told her quietly. 'Nothing compared with the cost of a man's life.

'Don't worry,' she reassured Anna as she saw her anxious face. '*You* won't be in any danger.'

No, maybe *she* wouldn't, Anna acknowledged as she watched Dee drive away ten minutes later, but what about Dee? Ridiculous though she knew other people would find it, in view of Dee's uncompromisingly self-assured attitude, Anna actually felt very protective towards her. No one could look into those tortoiseshell-coloured eyes and see, as she, Anna, had so briefly seen, the pain and anger that sometimes lurked there, without doing so.

And Anna knew all about pain and anger and, yes, there was guilt too. Emotions these women shared, but both chose to hide their pain from those around them.

Look for Anna's story in
LOVER BY DECEPTION.
Available soon from
Harlequin Presents.

HARLEQUIN PRESENTS®

invites you to see
how the other half marry in:

SOCIETY WEDDINGS

This sensational new five-book miniseries invites
you to be our VIP guest at some of the most talked-
about weddings of the decade—spectacular events
where the cream of society gather to celebrate the
marriages of dazzling brides and grooms in
breathtaking, international locations.

Be there to toast each of the happy couples:

Aug. 1999—**The Wedding-Night Affair**, #2044,
Miranda Lee

Sept. 1999—**The Impatient Groom**, #2054,
Sara Wood

Oct. 1999—**The Mistress Bride**, #2056,
Michelle Reid

Nov. 1999—**The Society Groom**, #2066,
Mary Lyons

Dec. 1999—**A Convenient Bridegroom**, #2067,
Helen Bianchin

Available wherever Harlequin books are sold.

HARLEQUIN®
Makes any time special ™

Coming Next Month

HARLEQUIN PRESENTS®

THE BEST HAS JUST GOTTEN BETTER!

#2067 A CONVENIENT BRIDEGROOM Helen Bianchin
(Society Weddings)
In her marriage of convenience to Carlo Santangelo, Aysha
knew she'd gain wealth, status and the sexiest husband ever!
Aysha loved her fiancé and wanted a real marriage, but would
Carlo give up his glamorous mistress...?

#2068 LOVER BY DECEPTION Penny Jordan
(Sweet Revenge/Seduction)
When Anna Trewayne lost her memory, she mistakenly
believed Ward Hunter to be a friend and lover. She'd
welcomed him into her arms...her bed...but what would
happen when her memory returned?

#2069 A MARRIAGE BETRAYED Emma Darcy
Kristy longed to find her natural family, but instead she found
Armand Dutournier, who wanted revenge for a betrayal she
hadn't committed. Did that mean she had a twin? Was he the
only lead to the family she yearned for?

#2070 THE YULETIDE CHILD Charlotte Lamb
(Expecting!)
Dylan had been thrilled when she'd married handsome
Ross Jefferson after a whirlwind romance. But she'd also
moved out of town and become unexpectedly pregnant.
Worse—her husband seemed to be having an affair....

#2071 MISTLETOE MISTRESS Helen Brooks
Joanne refused to have an affair with her sexy, arrogant
boss, Hawk Mallen. But then he offered her a dream
promotion—with one catch: she was at his command day
and night. Could she resist such a tempting proposal?

#2072 THE FAITHFUL WIFE Diana Hamilton
Jake and Bella, once happily married, have been separated a
whole year. Now Jake and Bella are tricked into spending
Christmas together. Isolated, they discover the passion is
still there—but can they overcome their past?